I0598296

# Entwined Heartstrings

# E.B. Sullivan

Publisher's Note:

This is a work of fiction. All names, characters, places, and events are the work of the author's imagination.

Any resemblance to real persons, places, or events is coincidental.

Solstice Publishing - www.solsticepublishing.com

# Chapter One
## Sam

$A$t high noon, I dashed from my office into the hallway and just managed to catch the elevator before the doors closed behind me. In my haste, my sneaker clad feet stepped on the other passenger's wing tipped shoes.

His arms caught me. "Hi, Sam. Looks like perfect timing." Jack asked. "Ready to join me for lunch?"

He was a defense attorney for the most prestigious firm in our city. Their swank offices were housed several floors above mine. He'd asked me out on numerous occasions, but I always turned him down. He was pleasant enough handsome too, but since we worked in the same building, I didn't want to risk becoming a topic of interest for the gossip pool.

His dreamy stare made me feel I was floating on air. Uncomfortable with my momentary attraction toward him, I extricated myself from his gentle grip.

The elevator glided to a stop.

We walked together to the rear exit and I said, "Not today."

"From your outfit my guess is you're taking the rest of the day off. Can I join you on your adventure?"

Knowing I looked out of place dressed in capris and a short sleeve cotton shirt I glanced at his well-tailored suit and giggled. "Don't think you'd enjoy tagging along to the wilderness with a pack of wild teenagers."

"If only you'd given me advance notice I would've cleared my calendar and gladly joined you. Maybe away from work we can get acquainted."

He stopped at a sporty BMW parked in the first row. Guessing he must've gotten here before dawn to secure the cherry space I admired his dedication, but thinking men usually had one thing in mind, I wondered if he was leaving his office to have a romantic rendezvous.

He waved his hand. "Have fun and stay safe."

Regardless of him seeming like a nice guy, even if we'd met under different circumstances my answer would've been the same. Years earlier, no longer wanting to waste my precious time I declared a moratorium on dating.

When I stepped outside, hot air engulfed me. Without wearing a pair of expensive high heels, it felt good to take carefree strides across the tacky asphalt. With my car in sight, I pressed the key fob to unlock its doors. I thought of popping the trunk to double check the few things I'd packed, but decided since I'd be gone for only a few days it didn't matter if I'd forgotten anything.

While I was pulling out of my spot, with a honk of his horn Jack drove by. Just for an instant, I caught a glimpse of his impish smile and doubted my decision to avoid socializing. Convincing myself he was probably a player, I shook my head dismissing any desire to become acquainted with him.

Eight short blocks away Trinity Church came into view. With its white facade and pointed steeple, it resembled my hometown chapel.

Taking me to services was one of the few activities my parents did as a couple. During Sunday morning family time, despite their image of a united pair, I couldn't deny their strained relationship.

In my youth, being in church brought me a sense of hope that one day they'd fall back in love.

By my teens, I realized my parents married because they were pregnant with me. Feeling shame and guilt they decided the right thing to do was to legitimize my birth.

Over the years, their bitterness for feeling forced to be together spilt out in disrespectful behaviors. Although they only gave lip service to what they called religious beliefs, rather than directing me away from God, their attitudes and actions brought me closer to Him.

I turned into a driveway flanked with Japanese maples. Their branches laden with purple leaves knocked against the roof of my car causing me to switch my attention from the past to the present.

In the spacious parking lot, I pulled my car into a spot designated for compacts.

While I retrieved my suitcase, two blankets, and a pillow, I couldn't believe I'd let my paralegal, Trudy, talk me into being a chaperone for the youth group's weekend camping trip.

Although part of the congregation for years, I chose not to mingle with other parishioners. My one and only intention of belonging to the parish centered on private worship.

I didn't mind when she'd asked me to contribute to the group's fundraiser.

A few weeks later, she graciously told me, "Thanks to generous donations, including your sizable one, all the members will be able to spend three nights in beautiful Yosemite National Park."

I didn't mind when she asked for a day off in order to have a four-day weekend to accompany the youths. I told her, "You can take that Thursday and Friday off with pay. Hope you have fun."

But when she approached me at four-thirty yesterday afternoon with a sheepish expression, I knew she was up to something.

Her words confirmed my suspicion. "I know it's last minute, but one of the volunteers came down with the flu leaving us short of adult supervision. Pastor said he'd rather cancel the trip than let the teens be placed in an unsafe situation."

"What does that have to do with me?"

"Please say you'll come along as a chaperone. We've made all the arrangements and every one's so excited. You wouldn't want disappointing so many young people on your conscience. Would you?"

"But I don't know anything about the wilderness. I wouldn't be of any use and my presence wouldn't reduce any possible risks to the teens."

"Mostly you'll stay at camp and help with meal prep. You'll just tag along on hiking trips, bringing up the rear, and ensuring no one gets lost. Without you we'll be short the minimum adult to child ratio." She blinked her beguiling hazel eyes. "Please. I'd think as a respected member of the parish you'd jump at the chance at helping its teens."

"But I don't know how to relate to kids."

"Most are almost adults. Besides all you have to do is think of how you felt and what you were interested in at their age."

Rather than remembering those hard years, I focused on the present. "But what about my schedule? I have appointments. I just can't up and leave."

"Remember, because I wasn't going to be here, you asked me not to arrange any meetings. You said you wanted a light day to catch up on a few things."

Realizing she wouldn't take no for an answer, I reluctantly agreed and shared my thought. "Trudy you're wasting your talents. You really should consider becoming a defense attorney. You're a natural."

The words defense attorney made me think of Jack. With powers of persuasion as sharp as a samurai's sword, it was obvious he really wasn't serious about wanting to date me or he'd have convinced me by now to go out with him. I sighed, grateful for not having bought into his flippant teasing.

Trudy brought me back to the moment by giving me a hug and saying, "I know you won't regret your decision."

As I approached the bus, the driver came toward me, took my belongings, stuffed them in the open compartment under the bus, and slammed the oversized door shut.

He followed me up the few steps and took his seat.

To my amazement, even though I was twenty minutes early, the bus looked full.

Trudy waved as I passed her seat. I didn't recognize any of the other passengers reminding me I didn't pay attention to members of our congregation.

Without another choice, I sat in the last row.

From my vantage point, I watched animated faces engaged in conversations.

Minutes passed.

With her hair in a ponytail looking like one of the teenagers, Trudy came to the front of the bus. "Quiet please. I have a few announcements."

She paused until the bus was silent.

"Since Marge is ill, we have Samantha, seated at the back of the bus, as a replacement chaperone."

Heads turned.

Eyes glared at me.

I felt my cheeks burn.

In the next breath, Trudy spouted a list of rules.

The driver shut the doors.

Trudy whispered in his ear before taking her seat.

He reopened the doors.

Minutes clicked by.

Engaged in chatter, the teens didn't seem to mind waiting.

When a teenage girl carrying a backpack, blanket, and pillow came aboard the bus, the driver closed the doors.

I checked my watch. It was fifteen minutes past our scheduled departure time.

The young lady kept her head down as she came down the narrow aisle, stowed her gear on the shelf over my seat, and sat in the empty place next to me.

With long, wavy blonde hair, blue eyes, and a slim body, she looked nothing like I did at her age.

During those awkward years, I was short, chubby, and had dull, frizzy brown hair. Yet, I couldn't shake a haunting feeling that she and I shared a common bond.

The driver started the engine and eased out of the parking lot.

I extended my hand to shake hers. "Hi. I'm Sam."

Rather than acknowledging me, the girl closed her eyes.

As if I, too, was a sensitive teenager, I felt awkward, out of place, and somewhat rejected.

# Chapter Two
## Charley

Why was this day going all wrong?

It started with me throwing up before I even got a chance to finish breakfast.

Just as I was leaving Mom said, "What's that on your shirt? When will you learn to eat like a lady?"

Good thing she noticed the stain instead of one of the kids in our group seeing it. If anyone would've guessed it was vomit, thinking I was sick, I would've been sent home.

Then what?

How would I ever get away?

With my stepfather, Mike, watching my every move, I'm practically a prisoner in his house.

He takes me to school, watches until I enter the building, and is waiting for me when I get out.

He's a deacon at our church. He and Mom met while she was doing volunteer work. To present a good image he insisted I attend youth group. Wanting to look like a good stepdad, he drives me to and from meetings.

This trip is my only chance to free myself from his tight grip.

Lucky for me Mom was angry with me this morning, because if she'd hugged me before I left, knowing I may never see her again, I might've burst into tears.

No matter how blind she is to the idiot she married I still love her. I've tried to protect her from his poundings, and foul mouth, but she always wants to convince me it was her fault he lost his temper or he had become enraged because he had one beer too many.

Today she yelled, "Go get changed. Your dad is waiting for you."

I wanted to shout back at her.

*He's not my dad. His name is Mike and he's a jerk.*
*My dad is dead.*

*If he were alive, he'd beat up your husband so bad the man would never walk again.*

I thought of the nights I imagined my dad taking punches at horrible Mike. The mere thought of it helped me get through the days.

Once I got in Mike's car reeking with the stench of stale smoke, he started to lecture me and drove so slowly I could've walked.

"Stay away from the boys.

"Don't be telling anyone about the games we play. If you do, like I told you before, I'll deny I ever touched you. More importantly, I'll make your mom suffer for you telling a pack of lies."

He grabbed my wrist and twisted it. "Get it sweetie?"

I got it all right.

I hoped he didn't see the glint in my eye as I thought, *This is the last time you'll ever lay your filthy hands on me.*

I took a seat at the back of the bus.

Relieved I had made it this far I closed my eyes and tried to calm my racing heart.

# Chapter Three
## Sam

Not the napping type I kept my eyes glued to the window, taking in the passing view.

We left Stockton's inner city via the freeway. Other than cars racing by, there wasn't anything interesting to see.

As the densely populated area faded in the distance the scenery transformed into rural vistas. I laughed at burnt grasses covering the low hills and expansive flatlands. Euphemistically, the label golden referred to their brown color. It along with golden sunsets, the Golden Gate Bridge, and past gold discoveries contributed to California being nicknamed the Golden State.

Along the way, I hoped to see splashes of the state's flower, golden poppies, but none came into view. Houses sparely dotted the terrain. Having always lived in a big city, I pondered what life would be like in the countryside. Due to isolation did folks act friendlier or did they choose to reside away from crowds in order to enjoy privacy?

The teenager sitting next to me mumbled. Her voice was faint and I didn't hear what she said.

Thinking she was speaking to me, I turned to her.

Sweat dotted her forehead. Her lips turned downward. Her fingers spread over her middle.

Guessing she was having a bad dream, I thought of waking her. But when I looked at her hands a second time, they seemed to be clutching her stomach making me think it might be feeling queasy.

When her eyes popped open, startled I jumped back.

She quickly rose and dashed into the restroom.

I couldn't help but hear her retching, confirming my guess about her having an upset stomach.

As the restroom door swung open, I peered out the window.

She shuffled to her seat.

By the time I turned, she once again appeared to be resting, her eyes shut, and her hands spread atop her midsection.

As a child, I had often gotten carsick especially if I sat in the back seat. When I told my parents, they'd tell me to open the window and stick my head out just in case I threw up. I'd asked my mom who was usually sitting in the front passenger seat to trade places with me, but she never did. She believed the only way to lick motion sickness was to outgrow it. Maybe she was right because as an adult I seldom felt queasy during car trips; however, I'd experienced many humiliating experiences before I reached that point.

Knowing how uncomfortable it felt to be nauseous and how embarrassing it was to throw up in public, I thought it might help the girl to change seats with Trudy.

I didn't get a chance to ask the teen, because she didn't open her eyes for the rest of the three-hour trip.

Unlike my mother, I was concerned and during most of the ride, I watched the youth. She was restless, uttered occasional moans and groans, but didn't move her hands.

When we pulled into the forested parking lot, she opened her eyes and caught me staring at her.

"You feeling okay?" I asked.

As if she hadn't heard me, she didn't answer.

After the others were off the bus, and retrieved their gear from the storage compartment she rose, collected her stuff, and made a slow exit.

While the teenagers branched off in pairs and groups of three, I trailed behind.

My former seatmate walked by herself.

I caught up to her and inhaled the pine scent. It reminded me of Christmas. My mom always insisted we have a freshly cut tree claiming she adored the fragrance. But from the moment my father carried it into the living room she complained about fallen needles. Several times a day she vacuumed around it. Her obsessive fastidiousness took away the delightful magic of its sparkling lights. In the first days of January when my father dragged it to the curb, I was happy to see it go.

I changed my focus and tried to make conversation with the teen. "After recent thunderstorms in the area, we're lucky to have such a clear day."

She didn't respond.

I persisted, "It's a little warm right now, but once the sun goes down, it'll be in the low fifties. Having a blanket will keep you cozy."

She quickened her pace creating a space between us.

Following her cue, I remained a few steps back for the short hike to the campground.

We passed rustic buildings—a small shop, restrooms, and showers. Rather than going off into the wilderness, we stopped at a large campsite. Two men from our church were setting up tents behind picnic tables. Two other men were starting a fire in a barbeque pit. Motor homes and campers filled the adjoining spaces.

The teens scurried about claiming their tents, but my seatmate was sitting alone at one of the tables.

I sat next to her.

"What's your name?" I asked.

She took a while to answer, "Charley."

"I'm Sam. What a coincidence, we both have names given to boys and girls."

Ignoring her blank expression, I continued talking. "Guess since we're the only two not scrambling for a place to sleep, we're going to share a tent."

She shrugged her shoulders.

Trudy's voice piped up. "Time to gather."

While the other teens sat around the weathered tables, Charley and I placed our belongings under a bench.

One teen told Charley, "Glad you decided to join us."

Charley nodded.

Someone else said, "We missed you at the last meeting."

The friendly youths addressed me.

"Nice to meet you."

I shook everyone's hand.

"Heard you're Trudy's boss."

I laughed. "Trudy's good at running things, including my office."

"She told us you're a successful attorney. What type of law do you practice?"

"My specialty is tax law."

Trudy interrupted us. "Please bow your heads."

After saying Grace, she announced, "Okay. Time to chow down."

We formed a line, took paper plates and filled them with hamburgers, chips, and cookies. Each person grabbed a soda or a bottle of water.

While devouring our food a hush descended. Sounds I hadn't noticed before sparked my attention. Rustling leaves seemed to set the tempo for birds chirping, humming almost serenading us with lilting songs.

After our meal, renewed energy sprang from the teens like a geyser. Most popped up and off the benches. Words showered down from their mouths, spraying the area with a cacophony of sounds. Wisely, a few chaperones took a sizable group on a hike.

I stayed at the campground to help clear the tables, clean cooking utensils, and prepare a late evening dinner.

While I learned the fascinating art of making cornbread shortcake in a cast iron pot over hot coals, Charley went into our tent and remained there until the chaperones served the cake topped with whipped cream, sprinkles, and fresh berries.

Later, I noticed although she sat with the group she didn't join in singing songs around the campfire. By now, I was certain she was suffering from emotional rather than physical pain.

As the wood crackled, I watched sparks rising up from the flames. They resembled fireflies flittering in the night air. With shimmering stars overhead and a gentle breeze, I tried to enjoy the peaceful ambiance.

The wind must have shifted, because smoke hit me square in the face. Along with its chocking aroma, worrisome thoughts of Charley's depressed state made it impossible for me to feel at ease.

Apart from the group, she was sitting with her legs drawn up to her chest. Perhaps she was cold. I wanted to suggest she move her chair closer to the roaring flame to soak up its warmth, but I didn't want to annoy her.

When it was time to turn in for the night, I gave Charley privacy. After I thought she was asleep, I entered the tent, wrapped myself in my blankets, and switched off my flashlight.

I lay there trying to rest, but wondering what was troubling my tent mate I couldn't relax.

# Chapter Four
## Charley

Finally, this Sam lady stopped jabbering.

She bugged me all day with do-gooder questions.

Her high-pitched voice asked.

"Did I feel okay?"

"Didn't I think it was a nice day?"

"Did I like the food?"

"Did I mind sharing a tent with her?"

It seemed she just couldn't take a hint.

She must be dense not to have seen all I wanted was to be alone. I'd hoped that far from the house no one would interrupt wonderful fantasies of being free.

What I really wanted was to have private time with my baby.

More and more each day I felt convinced I was carrying a baby girl.

I wanted to think of how pretty she'd be dressed in pink. I wanted to imagine counting her ten short toes and ten tiny fingers. I wanted to think about rocking her in my arms.

At home, if you could call it that, Mike breathed down my neck while I did homework or watched TV. He waited for me when I showered or used the bathroom. Early on, I threw a towel over the doorknob just in case he was peeking at me through the keyhole.

And during the night, I never knew when he'd sneak into my room and...

I didn't want to think of those awful times. I wanted to think about the future.

Of course, Sam would never suspect I was pregnant. It wouldn't cross her prissy mind that a fifteen-year old was knocked up by her demented deacon stepfather.

All day long, I tried to focus.

I needed time to think, to observe the layout of the campsite, and plan my escape.

In a few hours, I'd be out of here. I'd be on my way to freedom. I planned to protect my baby from her wicked father by getting her far away from his filthy reach.

I won't let him spread lies about me saying I slept around. I won't let the authorities take my daughter and give her to strangers to adopt or foster parents who might hurt her.

What I intended to do was shower my infant with love. As she grew, I'd be there to listen to every word she said. I was never going to be too busy, too brainwashed, too intimidated to forsake my precious child.

Kind of ironic actually. My mom insisted I take this lame trip.

She told me, "Your dad and I need a little alone time to get romance back in our marriage. I'm going to surprise him by taking Friday off and booking a cabin in Clear Lake. After a day of floating on the calm water, fishing, and drinking some beers he'll be in the mood for love."

Her words made me sick. Mike didn't know the first thing about love. He was all about lust. He was gross. He viewed child porn on his computer and ever since he married my mom a year ago, he grabbed at me whenever he had the chance.

After their whirlwind courtship of two short months, my mind couldn't wrap around her decision to become his wife.

My mom gushed, "Did you know the odds of a forty year woman getting a marriage proposal were as rare as winning the lottery?"

I pointed out, "But, Mom, Mike's no prize. He's unemployed, drinks too much, and is a slimeball."

She shut me up. "He loves me and what's more I love him. He's a good Christian man and generously wants to raise you like his own."

No matter my objections, one day while I was at school, she eloped with him to Reno. From then on, my life had been hell.

How could she want that lazy, pig. While she worked at a warehouse lifting and pushing heavy boxes, he sat on the couch eating, waiting for the hour he could pick me up from school and begin tormenting me.

Every time, I asked her why he didn't get a job, do laundry, cook, or clean she reminded me, "Poor man suffers from severe back pain. It takes all his strength to drive you everywhere you need to go. And what's more, he seldom complains."

I wondered if my mom was blind and deaf or just plain dumb. Everything from his excess weight to his deranged mind was wrong with this strong and powerful guy.

Lucky for me, in her delusional state she felt excited about the prospects of having a mini vacation with Mike. In her elated mood, she gave me spending money to buy gear and new clothes.

"Mike can take you to the mall."

I never asked him for a ride. Didn't she know if Mike knew I had a few dollars he'd take them from me, buy street drugs, and spend the night hurting us?

I stashed every penny. Together with that cash and what I stole from Mom's saving jar, I figure I'd have enough money to pay for things until I could find a job.

At dawn, after being awake for most of the night, I listened to Sam's breathing. She was in a deep sleep.

Thanks to Mike, I had learned how to move around without making a sound.

It was easy to slip out of my blanket, grab my backpack, and hightail it out of the campground without waking her.

# Chapter Five
## Sam

My eyelids slowly opened. Taking in the dimness, I realized it was too early to wander around the campsite. Cuddled up in the warm blankets, I listened to birdcalls. Although I knew nothing about winged creatures, I could tell from their high pitched to deep calls there were several varieties lighting in nearby trees. To my surprise, their combined sounds as if different notes of a symphony created a soothing melody.

I was glad Trudy talked me into spending the weekend in Yosemite. It had been a long time since I'd been in the forest. I recalled hiking with my ex-boyfriend, Cameron. Along with a group of friends, we spent the day in Muir Woods. After the long drive, we strolled trails and talked for hours. I liked feeling the softness under my feet, breathing the refreshing scented air, and seeing the magnificent coastal redwoods.

While wandering through the lush surroundings with Cameron, I felt drawn to him. I wanted to believe he was different from other guys. I wanted to believe his respectful behaviors were sincere.

He suggested on our next trip into the wilderness we sleep under the stars, but there wasn't a next time. Two weeks later, thinking I'd surprise him with a cake for his birthday, I went to his condo. Turned out the surprise was on me. I found him in the arms of another woman.

Since then, more than four years ago, I hadn't dated. Working long hours, and usually only meeting men who were clients or coworkers, made it easy to be a social hermit. My one indulgence was to fantasize about an idealized man genuinely kind, smart, accomplished, and handsome. As long as my musing centered on a fictional character he could remain the perfect eligible bachelor.

As I turned over, fully intending to fall back to sleep, unconsciously I checked on Charley.

She wasn't there.

I stood up and scanned the tent. Her blanket and pillow were in a heap, but her backpack was gone.

I told myself she was probably taking a shower. Yet, a foreboding added to my jitters. I chided myself for not telling Trudy about Charley's obvious depression.

Without changing my wrinkled clothes I flung a blanket over my shoulders, I left the tent and glanced at the tables. No one was sitting on any of the benches.

A pungent stench made my nose involuntarily scrunch up.

A chaperone standing over a blazing grill said, "Sorry. Good thing the lighter fluid's toxic fumes will burn off in a few minutes."

I shot him a smile before leaving the area.

I headed for the restrooms. All doors were open revealing empty stalls. Next, I went into the women's shower cabin. Two chaperones were talking while combing their wet hair.

I interrupted them. "Have you seen Charley?"

They shook their heads.

I returned to the campsite. Another chaperone was pulling egg cartons out of a cooler.

"Have you seen Charley this morning?" I asked.

"Not yet."

"Which tent is Trudy in?"

She pointed to one on the end.

Without hesitation, I entered it, knelt down, and tapped Trudy on her shoulder.

As if my nudge was part of a dream, she didn't respond.

I whispered in her ear, "Trudy, I have to tell you something."

Her tent mate, one of the teenage girls turned over.

Trudy's eyes blinked open. A bit groggy she asked, "What are you doing here?"

"Charley's gone."

"She must be out on a morning run."

"With her backpack?"

"She's probably taking a shower."

"I've already checked, but couldn't find her."

"Don't worry. She has to be nearby."

"Didn't you notice how strange she was acting yesterday? She was quiet and didn't mingle."

"That's the way she usually behaves." She lifted her head. "Go back to bed or help prepare breakfast. I'm certain Charley will return in no time."

Regardless of what Trudy said, I was worried. I was sure something was wrong, very wrong.

I returned to my tent, stuffed my wallet and cell phone in my pockets, and put on my jacket.

Before I left the campsite, I grabbed a few energy bars from a box filled with snacks. I also took two water bottles.

I told the chaperone whisking eggs in a large bowl, "I'm going to look for Charley."

"Just make sure you're both back by the time breakfast is served."

I hoped to do just that.

# Chapter Six
## Charley

A few days before the trip, I was a mess of nerves. Needing to do something, I visited Yosemite's webpage on one of the library's computers. Even though Mike allowed me to use his laptop to do homework assignments, I dared not do any research on his PC. I didn't trust him not even for a minute. He probably encouraged me to go online because it was one more way he could check up on me. He wanted to know everything about me all the time.

He'd say, "Tell me what you're thinking."

Of course, I kept my opinions to myself. If I told him the truth about how much I despised him, he probably would've killed me by now.

He often asked, "Why don't you have a Facebook page?"

I wondered if he wanted me on social media so he could check out girls at my school. Or maybe he wanted to know if I had a secret boyfriend.

Yosemite's webpage had maps of all the park's trails. Even though I didn't know exactly where our youth group would be camping, and didn't want to arouse suspicion by asking, I could see that several trails intercepted and could lead to different ways to leave the park. Just knowing there were many exits, gave me confidence.

While I silently tiptoed out of the tent, I thought, with any luck, I'd be too far away to track before anyone noticed I was gone.

At the trailhead, in the dim light, I studied the map. I wished I had thought to buy a compass. If anyone was looking for me, it might be safer to travel in the woods than to stay on trails. I wondered why I hadn't thought of that before leaving Stockton. Thinking there were lots I hadn't thought of made me shiver.

Fearing I could get lost if I tried to take an unmarked route, I decided to stick to my original plan and started my journey.

Soon, my empty stomach churned. I stopped to search my backpack for a box of crackers. But it was too late to prevent the dry heaves from making me double over.

Minutes later, with the most recent bout of morning sickness behind me, I felt a bit better.

I told my little one, "Hope time rushes by. I'm tired of feeling nauseous. But most of all, I can't wait to meet you."

Not wanting to waste any more precious time, I munched crackers as I moved along.

The path surprised me. It wasn't straight and it kept climbing. Since I'd never been in the wilderness before, I just assumed walking around the park would be as easy as strolling through the mall.

When my dad was alive, he took us on a few vacations. One was to Disneyland. I was almost five and don't really remember much except it was fun.

We also went to the beach. He carried me on his shoulders into the water, I giggled when waves splashed my body. But my favorite thing to do was to play in the sand.

I still smiled when I remembered him asking me to bury him. He was a good-natured guy. When I accidently kicked sand in his face, he just laughed.

My dad was so kind and patient, so different from Mom.

He liked to bring me little gifts, but my mom would tell him, "Stop wasting our money. She already has a room full of junk."

She was always nervous and wanted things just so. She was always cleaning something and too busy to be with me. She kept telling me not to make messes. She said I made too much noise and was always giving her a headache.

After Dad died, she seemed angry all the time. Almost every day she whined about not having enough money.

"Didn't I give you lunch money last week? Why do you need more?"

"Don't tell me your shoes are too tight already."

"What do you think? Money grows on trees."

"No. We can't afford to take a vacation."

I hung my head in guilt thinking maybe what Mike did to me was punishment for all the times I wished Mom had died instead of Dad.

Still, I wished he were alive.

I rubbed my tummy. "Little one, maybe God gave me you so I could be as great a parent as my dad was."

The sounds of footfalls frightened me. Someone was coming. I darted off the trial into the woods. In a panic, not looking where I was going I tripped over a log.

Even with long sleeves and long pants, I felt stinging scraps.

Too much in a hurry to check on my wounds, I got up and headed for a large tree stump. I slithered down to hide.

From its side I could see a glimpse of the path.

I watched and waited all the while hoping whoever it was hadn't heard my fall and couldn't hear my loud heartbeats.

A man in shorts ran by.

I sighed with relief and whispered to my babe, "We're okay. It was only an early bird getting his run in before breakfast."

# Chapter Seven
## Sam

As I rushed away from the campsite, I questioned what I was doing. I knew nothing about the area and less about finding my way through a forest. I glanced at the sneakers I'd purchased the night before. I laughed thinking this would be the last time I'd see them clean and I hoped these highly recommended shoes wouldn't pinch my feet as they ventured on a dirt path for the first time.

I came to trailhead markers and reviewed the choices. There was a less than a mile-looped trail.

I shook my head. If Charley had taken the short loop trail, she would've been back by now. And if she wanted to escape, she would've taken a different route.

Another trail zigzagged to a waterfall. I doubted that was her destination.

I traced a longer trail with my finger. At its endpoint was another campground. Beyond the facilities was a park exit. When I saw an arrow pointing in the direction of a town, my heart raced. I thought if Charley was running away she'd take the longer path and leave the park.

Walking at a quick pace, I occasionally called her name, but there was no reply.

The stillness astounded me. At every turn, it seemed as if I was the only creature roaming these woods. Knowing that was impossible, I wondered if my movements or my scent caused the wildlife to take cover.

Had Charley heard me? Was she hiding somewhere close by?

I thought, *Where would a teenager go?*

I tried taking Trudy's advice of remembering myself as a teenager.

My guess was Charley was in her mid-teens.

Sixteen had to be the worst year of my life.

My parents abruptly announced they were divorcing, because my dad had a lover. The following week he moved out of our house and out of the country. He announced he'd taken a job opportunity he couldn't pass up in his company's Tokyo branch.

During their freshman college year, my parents had a casual but intimate relationship. Both wanting to date others, they were about to break up when they discovered they were pregnant with me. They agreed it was best to leave school, get jobs, and marry. From then on resentments grew. While working full time to support us, it took my father eight years of night classes to earn his bachelor's degree. My mother sacrificed her education to be a stay at home mom. Throughout their marriage, they presented a public image of being the perfect couple. Privately they had difficulty being civil to each other.

Yet, when my father left her, my mother was devastated. According to her, his affair caught her completely off guard.

Spoiled by my dad taking care of her financially, my mom hadn't worked since before my birth. Without him and with a bruised ego, she threw herself at one man after another.

Despite my father's flowery words of love, I felt abandoned. He called every week, but our chats were brief. It was as if he was only checking in out of duty rather than being truly interested in me.

Upon his invitation, that summer I traveled to Japan hoping my dad would shower me with attention. To my great disappointment, I quickly realized my reason for being there was to fulfill his two month a year court ordered visitation. Rather than taking vacation days, he worked overtime. He'd made provisions for me to attend a day camp at the international school. On weekends, his girlfriend was constantly with us. She was someone he had worked with in the states. Apparently, they'd been having an affair for over a year. They made plans, requested transfers, and left their spouses at almost the same time.

Following my parents' divorce, my mother's chosen job was to find another husband. Her criteria list included two items. He had to be solvent and be willing to support us. Nothing else seemed to matter. She dated alcoholics, shady businessmen, and arrogant guys. I tried talking to her, telling her she deserved better, but with sights on her quest, she didn't listen to me.

While I was in Tokyo, she married a man I hadn't met.

On the way home from the airport, Mom broke the news. "I have a fantastic surprise." She flashed a diamond wedding band. "You'll be so happy to learn I found you a new dad. He's such a fine man and a terrific husband." She went on and on comparing him to my father. She bragged about her current husband's lucrative business, his vacation home on Florida's east coast where they'd honeymooned, and his pledge to provide for my future.

The minute she introduced me goosebumps covered my arms and I felt nervous.

Her husband had beady eyes, slick hair, and was dressed weird. His moist warm hands clutched mine. He squeezed them so tight I told him to let go of me. When I turned to leave, my mom reprimanded me for being rude. With tears in my eyes, I ran into my room wishing I could run far from home.

*Was that Charley's desire?*

I put myself back into that dreadful September.

The night I returned home, my stepdad came into my bedroom. Thinking I was asleep, he pulled back my covers. He must've stood there staring at me.

Suddenly, I felt his hands grope my breasts.

I started to scream but he silenced me by pressing his palm over my opened mouth.

Next morning when I told my mother, she defended him. "You know how you twist in your sleep and kick off your blankets. He was merely trying to fix your covers in order to keep you warm."

From then on, just like Charley, I was sullen, quiet, and reclusive.

If I'd had the chance to take a three-hour bus ride from home to a forest, I would've hiked a trail leading to another exit from the park. I would've stayed in town, pretended to be eighteen, and looked for work.

A dreadful thought occurred to me, *Maybe Charley wasn't sick to her stomach because she sat in the back of the bus.*

*Maybe she felt sick because she was pregnant.*

That would explain her retching, moaning, groaning, and holding her hands over her middle.

Whether my guess was wrong or right I felt compelled to find her.

While I trudged along, I remembered reading this trail was supposed to be moderately strenuous. Why was I uncomfortable? I'd already downed one bottle of water. Yet, my mouth felt as if cotton balls stuffed every inch of it.

Trying not to think of me, I thought about Charley. If she already reached the town, she could've hitchhiked to a bus depot. If so, she could be in another state by morning.

I hoped I could catch up to her and convince her to return without anyone knowing she tried to run away.

I reasoned. Surely, she wouldn't have left while it was dark. Carrying her backpack, she'd travel at a slower pace than I would move. I concluded she couldn't be too far in front of me and I'd be able to overtake her within an hour or two.

But who was I kidding? She was younger than I was by at least fifteen years. I had a sedentary job and I wasn't accustomed to hiking. And if I was correct about her running away, she had a lot more incentive to hurry than I did.

I tried to give myself a pep talk. I knew I had excellent endurance. To do the best for my clients and meet demanding deadlines I pulled many all nighters. My pattern was the more I worked the more energy I had.

If Charley was pregnant, she might tire easily and would need to take rest breaks.

Inspired, I pushed forward on the trail taking quicker steps.

The switchbacks climbed uphill. My breaths dived deep into my chest as if they were searching for every molecule of oxygen. I felt my feet slowing and I understood the words moderately strenuous meant the trail had a steep upward grade. Regardless of the discomfort, hoping I wasn't heading in the wrong direction, I kept moving.

# Chapter Eight
## Charley

A sharp cramping like someone squeezing my gut overpowered me. My body folded over before sinking to the dusty ground.

Along with the intense pain, terror spread to every part of me.

Tears drenched my face.

*How can I be a mother when I feel like a frightened little child?*

While trying to quiet my sobs, my feet felt weighed down with a strange heaviness making it impossible to stand.

*Maybe I had moved too fast, traveled too far.*

Not wanting anything to happen to my baby, I thought it best to wait awhile before going on. Truth was I didn't have the strength to go anywhere.

I closed my eyes.

A grotesque thought clouded my mind.

*Was there something wrong with my pregnancy?*

*Was my child in danger?*

My head moved from side to side. My lips reassured my babe, "You have to stay alive. I can't live without you. I love you so much."

I wanted to wrap her in a soft pink blanket.

I wanted to rock her in my arms.

I longed to hear her coo.

Despite wishful thinking, along with a cold sweat fear poured out of me like water gushing from an open faucet.

"Please, please don't leave me," I begged her.

I willed myself to be still.

Sometime later, the pain went from acute to a dull ache.

I tried to stand, but couldn't.

Gripping my stomach, I managed to get on my knees. I crawled away from the path and slowly made my way into the sheltered woods.

Suddenly, a sensation warned me to take it easy.

I felt hot, clammy, and very dizzy.

Trembling, I slipped off my backpack, stretched out on the ground, and closed my eyes.

I knew I wasn't moving, but I felt like either the world or I was spinning faster and faster out of control.

A long while passed before the rapid turning stopped and the pain subsided.

I told my daughter, "All I need is a few minutes of sleep. Then I'll whisk you away from here to our new home."

With one hand, I rubbed my stomach.

I crossed two fingers on my other hand.

Not wanting to pass anxiety to my infant, I hummed one of my favorite tunes.

# Chapter Nine
## Sam

While exerting my body to the max, my mind raced lots faster than my feet. My brain interpreted my surroundings as a continuous stream of blurred greenery.

It occurred to me, if Charley were an avid hiker who could follow a compass, she would avoid taking any trails. I tried to peer into the repetitive denseness. Every turn looked exactly like ones behind me. Walled in by brush and trees it felt impossible to find anyone who wanted to remain hidden.

Even if I stumbled upon her, if she wanted to run away, why would she agree to return to the campsite with me? Why would she listen to me when I was a stranger and didn't have authority over her?

A scenario crossed my mind. What if she'd arranged for a boyfriend to meet her at the park's exit? He could have a car and drive her far from here before I reached her. But it didn't make sense for someone to meet her in Yosemite when it would've been easier for a boyfriend to pick her up before she boarded the bus.

Sooner than I expected the sun beat down. Trying to stop my eyes from watering, I squinted and wished I'd worn sunglasses. Sweat drenched my back. I stripped off my jacket and tied it around my waist. I wished I'd thought to put sunscreen on my face, arms, and legs.

Assuming campers were early risers and eager to be active I'd hoped I could ask an approaching individual if he or she had passed a teenager. Surprisingly, I hadn't encountered anyone on the trial.

No matter what was going on with Charley, I chided myself for abandoning my role as chaperone. As a responsible adult, I had no right going off on what was probably a wild goose chase. It was possible Charley hadn't run away. She may've taken a quick stroll and by now was back at our campground.

I laughed realizing if I lumbered into camp and saw her sitting at a picnic table despite being sunburned, I'd be pleased I'd gone into panic mode for nothing.

My next thought erased my glee.

Something inside me told me to trust my instincts. From experience, I knew my intuition was usually pretty close to being on target.

I had a habit of studying people and developed highly developed observation skills. In my law practice, I was able to read my clients' cues accurately. Their body language sometimes as slight as a shifting stare or a hesitant movement made them seem transparent. I often confronted them when I thought they were less than truthful. After expressing indignation, most clients concurred with my analysis.

Charley had sent several signals. She was depressed. No matter who had fathered her child by the way she caressed her belly, I guessed she wanted to protect her infant.

Reflecting in the sunlight a glossy wrapper on the side of the trail caught my attention.

*Was it a beacon pointing my way?*

Of course, many people walked this path. Anyone at anytime could've dropped it, but I held onto the hope Charley unconsciously let it slip out of her hand while she munched breakfast.

Without slowing my pace, I kept turning my head alternately craning my neck to see what was beyond the path. No longer concentrating on the few feet in front of me I tripped. In an awkward attempt to regain my balance my arms flayed wildly before I came crashing down. My hands skidded in the dirt. Its rocky surface pricked my shins. My left ankle screamed with pain.

After struggling up to a sitting position, hoping I hadn't broken a bone I tried rubbing away the intense throbbing.

Like a fool wasting time pampering and comforting myself, I ate an energy bar and sipped water from the second bottle I'd intended to give to Charley.

When I tried to stand, a stabbing sensation in my tender ankle caused me to hop on my other foot.

Determined to find Charley, I hobbled off the path in search of a makeshift walking stick.

Covered with peeling bark a fallen limb seemed to fit the bill. I scooped it up and examined it. Looking quite sturdy, I leaned on it pleased to discover it could bear my weight.

Favoring my right leg, I used my left one to keep me erect as I continued to trek ahead.

# Chapter Ten
## Charley

Covered in sweat and shivering I woke in a panic. I worried someone at the campsite would realize I was missing.

Would a group of teens come looking for me?

To calm myself, I stopped thinking of negative possibilities. At least I wasn't in pain and might be able to move fast enough to make up for lost time.

With my backpack securely in place, I carefully climbed over brush and made my way to the path.

Not sure which way to turn I headed left.

Before long, I noticed an imprint in the dirt. I turned over my foot and compared the footprint with the sole of my sneaker. They were a match, which meant I was heading back to the campground.

I resisted an urge to scream, "Why was everything going wrong? Why wasn't God helping me?"

Fearing I'd never get away, I spun round and walked as quickly as my feet could move.

The weight of my pack made my shoulders ache. I tried pushing the straps to the side, but the soreness continued. I thought of leaving it, but knew I needed the few things I'd taken with me.

No matter how bad I felt, I had to keep going. I had to get far from here. I had to save my baby from Mike.

Suddenly, I heard a sound ahead of me. My heart felt like it was about to jump out of my chest. My brain warned me I couldn't risk anyone seeing me. Knowing I had to hide I darted into the woods and slithered down behind a wide tree trunk.

A tapping noise grew louder.

I felt a bit relieved thinking it was a solitary hiker, who would soon pass me.

Abruptly the sound stopped.

I slowly moved my head until I could see the path.

When I spied Sam, my hand pressed into my lips to stifle a gasp.

*What was she doing here?*

*Was she out for an innocent walk or was she searching for me?*

She was just standing leaning on a long piece of wood.

My head jerked back behind the tree.

*Why wasn't she moving? Had she stopped because she heard me?*

Her moaning made me wonder if she was injured.

As I peeked out again, she threw down the stick and sank to the ground.

Her hands covered her eyes. Her sobs grew louder.

*Was she in pain?*

I told myself not to care about Sam and use this opportunity to get away.

A flock of cawing birds flew overhead. Were they telling me to follow them? I gazed at them envying their ability to fly. If I had wings, I'd be free to find a new home, free of the monster my mother loved, free to raise my baby in peace.

The birds faded into the blue sky leaving me alone.

I, too, had to take flight. I pressed on slithering under trees and climbing over clumps of grasses.

After a few minutes, wanting to move faster, and fearing I'd get lost in the forest I made my way back to the trail.

With each step, I felt more and more ashamed of leaving Sam crying. What if she was badly hurt? What if she'd had a heart attack?

I told myself someone would come along and help her, but so far, I'd only seen the one runner.

What if she couldn't get up?

What if an animal attacked her?

What if no one came along and she had to spend the cold, dark night by herself?

With each step, my conscience gnawed at me.

What kind of person would I be if I didn't offer to help Sam?

If she died out here alone in the wilderness, I'd never forgive myself for being selfish.

I realized if I didn't check on her, I'd be a terrible example for my child.

"Darn you, Sam," I muttered as I turned around and headed in her direction.

When she came into view I shouted, "Is that you, Sam? Do you need help?"

She answered, "I'm so happy to see you. Are you okay?"

When I reached her, I sat at her side. "I'm fine. Just out for a hike. Want some water? How about crackers?"

I swung my backpack into my lap, pulled out a plastic bottle and offered it to her. "Looks like you're pretty uncomfortable. What's wrong?"

She took a long drink before answering. "I must've sprained my ankle."

As she pulled down her sock, I saw her ballooned, discolored skin. "It could be broken." I ripped open a packet of crackers. As she nibbled on one I told her, "You best not walk on it." I lied, "I was almost at the end of the trail when I decided to return to the campsite." I pointed. "I'll run back in that direction to get you medical attention. It'll be quicker than returning to our group."

Sam clutched my wrist. "You're running away. Aren't you?"

I tried to look surprised. "What gave you that idea?"

"You're running away from your family, your boyfriend, society?"

"You must be delirious." With my free hand, I felt her forehead. "I'm not even sixteen yet and I've never been on a date and I certainly don't have a boyfriend."

I sighed. "You're very warm. Too much sun and too much pain, is my guess."

I tried to free my wrist, but Sam held on tight as she said, "Help me up. If I can lean on you, I'm sure I can make it to the end of the trail."

Feeling I had no other choice, I did as she asked.

# Chapter Eleven
## Sam

Trying not to put too much of my weight on Charley, using my good leg, I hopped down the trail. Dust and debris scattered in my wake.

Instead of asking her a host of questions, I talked about my past. I told her about my parents divorcing.

She didn't comment and probably didn't care, but I continued talking.

"My father was so obsessed with his lover, he almost ignored me. He made it clear I wasn't welcome in his life. Feeling hurt by his rejection, I cried during the long flight from Japan. At home, my mother surprised me by introducing me to her new husband. He was a stranger I'd never met, a man who turned out to be a worthless slimy pervert."

Charley tighten her grip on my shoulder, but she didn't say a word.

While we continued in silence, images of my wretched stepdad hovering over me spun in my mind. I could almost feel his demonic eyes staring at me. The thought of his creepy touch made me shudder.

"You okay?" Charley asked.

Without thinking I shared, "An appalling memory of my stepdad just flashed in my mind." I stopped myself from describing a scene I'd forgotten until that moment. His naked body was straddling mine.

Uncontrollable tremors rumbled through me and threatened to unleash an out of control tempest.

"You sure you're all right? If you need to rest, we can stop."

"I'm fine." There was a harsh edge in my voice. "I'm sorry. I didn't mean to snap at you."

She didn't respond.

Every throb in my ankle reminded me of my stepfather's repeated trusts hurting me. With one of his huge hands covering my mouth, I couldn't cry out. The realization of him violating me beyond what I'd previously remembered caused my body to go limp. I fell out of Charley's grasp and dropped in a heap to the ground.

Helpless, confused, and afraid described my feelings.

Charley bent down next to me and took my hand.

A part of me wanted to confide in her, but since she really was a child, I didn't dare tell her about my horrific recollections.

Perhaps in a way of distracting me, to my surprise, Charley shared, "After my dad died, my mom changed. Like your mom, she was desperate to remarry. She settled for a real... what you called your stepdad. Mine is the same."

What she hinted at validated my suspicions. I feared her horrid stepdad had molested her. Worst of all, he'd impregnated her.

A fury seethed within me. Anger like hot steam rose and burnt my throat. I didn't think I could speak without spewing forth rage. I took a few deep breaths. My wrath wouldn't help Charley. As a mature adult, I had to push my past and present ire aside. I had to let Charley share her story if or when she felt safe to do so.

After stuffing my teenage-self back in its hidden hiding place, I spoke in a grownup voice. "Thank you for letting me rest. I'm ready to walk."

With her help, I got back on my feet. With an arm draped over her shoulders, I limped along.

With each switchback, the path repeated a pattern of going up then down. Regardless of Charley's presence, the repetitive motion like a metronome's beat put me in a hypnotic trance and triggered images of my stepdad rising and falling on top of me.

Sweat poured over me. More than physical fatigue, I felt emotionally drained. Yet I kept walking.

I tried to stop the memories, but they kept bombarding my mind. As if floating out of my body I watched sixteen-year old me from a distance. I viewed the unfolding scene as if I was viewing a make believe movie about a fictitious character.

I saw me lying in bed sleeping.

My stepdad came into my room and ordered me not to cry out.

Wide-eyed I watched him undressing. With his repulsive nakedness, he pounced on me. Under his great weight, he looked at me. As if he enjoyed me struggling, he grinned. Even before he pushed his hand over my opened mouth, I tried to scream but not a single sound came out.

Horrified I laid parlayed as he took off my pajamas. My fear seemed to excite him. It felt as if he had several hands all of which were touching every inch of me. It felt like his fist pounded my most private part, but I did nothing to stop him.

I didn't want to accept what he was really doing. I didn't want to believe he was inside me. I wanted to pretend I was having a nightmare.

I willed myself to detach from my body lying there with him on top of me doing vile things. I went far away mentally. I imagined I was stretched out on a beach with the sun warming me as I peacefully slept.

I thought I'd escaped him, but the smell of his putrid breath brought me back to my bed. His powerful tongue pried open my mouth wiggled down my throat and made me gag.

I was so young, so innocent, all alone, a victim of his wickedness. While my mother was busy treating him like royalty, she failed to notice me slipping deeper into a hardened shell. Sad and afraid I couldn't concentrate on my schoolwork. I tuned out my teachers' voices. Rather than writing, I scribbled gibberish symbols in my notebooks. I found it impossible to solve even the simplest math problem. My grades tumbled. Maybe not wanting to hear the truth, my mother never asked me what was wrong.

At nightfall, I tried to hide under my bed or in my closet. His long, strong arms reached for me. Sometimes he lifted me and threw me on my bed. Other times he did his terrible deeds with me on the floor or against a wall, or in between my hanging clothes. He laughed, and said he enjoyed playing hide-and-seek.

When my period was late, panic like a bear trap seized me. Day after day, I thrashed about but couldn't get free of the thought of being pregnant.

During my dad's routine scheduled call, after he said hello, words poured from my lips. "Mom's husband planted his baby in me."

I don't remember what he said, but that afternoon without talking much my mother drove hours from home to a boarding school. On the way, instead of stopping at a physician's office for me to have an examination or going to the police station to report my stepdad's heinous crime she went to the mall and bought me pajamas, clothes, and underwear.

Within days of arriving at the school's protective walls, my body resumed its normal functions. Relieved I wasn't pregnant, my mind started to forget and blocked out the events that led me to a safe haven. During the first few months, I buried myself in books and excelled in my classes. Although several girls befriended me and confided in me about their past abuses, I was too ashamed to tell anyone my deepest darkest secret. Eventually I joined the teens in fun activities and happily completed high school with honors.

Charley's voice brought me back to the moment. "Was he... did he... did your stepfather ever... hit you."

Without considering the appropriateness of telling her the truth about the malevolent man I blurted, "No, but he did worse things to me."

Despite her silence, her stiffen body expressed the truth. I asked her, "Want to tell me about your stepdad?"

Minutes passed.

As if we were two adolescent girlfriends she replied, "First tell me about yours."

I swallowed back my rage wondering how I could maturely discuss the delicate topic of my molestation with a teenager.

She said, "Sorry for being out of line, being too personal."

I tried to choose my words carefully. I tried to keep my voice free from emotion. "It began on my first night home from Japan. I was exhausted, upset, and went to bed early.

"When I first felt a draft and claws squeezing my breasts I thought I was having a bad dream.

"My eyes popped open. In the moonlit room my mother's foul husband was jeering at me." Skipping the graphic details, I said, "After he... He left, but made other nightly visits."

Words poured out of Charley's mouth. "My stepdad is a mean, mean man. He's hit my mother more times, than I can count. He's given her black eyes and broken her ribs."

She started sobbing.

I stopped moving, turned, and embraced her. Without taking one hand away from her waist, I stroked her hair with my other hand and said, "You poor, innocent child."

She looked into my eyes, "What about you? What else did you stepdad do?"

I swallowed a lump of realized horror. "You'd be the age of my child if I became pregnant from my stepfather's abuses."

Charley whispered, "Did you tell your mother? Did she stop him?"

"Yes I told her, but she didn't believe me. She said I was imagining things. She said, because I was a restless sleeper and tossed off my covers my stepdad stopped in my room each night to straighten out my blankets."

Charley pulled out of my embrace. As if disconnected from herself her words shared. "I didn't dare tell my mom. My stepdad threatened to strangle me then kill my mother if I didn't obey him. To stop him from hurting us more, I just let him do whatever he wanted. I just did whatever he told me to do." In the next breath she asked, "When did it end for you?"

"I told my dad. He put me in a boarding school. I haven't been home since. Yea I see my mom now and then, but I don't go to her house because she's still married to the despicable man. She's respected my wishes and hasn't pushed me to see her husband."

"I don't have a dad to save me. Mine died a long time ago. That's why I have to run away. You understand. Don't you?"

"Yes, but you have other options."

"How can you say that? You know I can't go back there."

She let out a harrowing scream and her body fell against mine.

While helping her lie on the ground I asked, "What's wrong?"

She gripped her middle and groaned.

I couldn't help but notice blood staining her pants.

Charley screamed, "Don't let my baby die."

I held her hands. "I'll go get help."

"Don't leave me."

I stroked her forehead. "I'm right here."

Her eyes closed.

I removed my cell phone from my pocket, but wasn't able to get a signal. Nonetheless, I pressed 911 repeatedly.

Hoping for guidance, I prayed for a miracle.

# Chapter Twelve
## Charley

The sound of a motor approaching made my eyes pop open and my heart pump with fear.

*Had someone heard me scream?*

*Would they take me to a hospital and keep my baby?*

I told Sam, "You don't need me anymore. I have to get away to save my child."

When I attempted to lift my torso, a sharp pain in my gut pushed me back on the hard ground.

With her face close to mine, she covered me with her jacket. "You're very cold. You need a doctor."

I wanted to protest, but knew she was right. I squeezed her fingers and stared into her eyes. "Please make them save my baby."

She nodded, but didn't make any promises.

A vehicle stopped in front of us. A uniformed woman approached.

Sam spoke up, "Charley needs medical attention. She's a few months pregnant."

The woman addressed me. "We're almost at the Fallen Pines campsite. Think you can ride in my vehicle?"

"I think so."

The stranger and Sam helped me stand. In the next instant, the strong woman lifted me into the front passenger seat.

Sam scooted next to me. I leaned into her allowing her weight to hold me up. She assured me, "You're going to be all right."

I heard the woman whispering into an oversized cell phone.

She told me, "An ambulance is on its way. It's only a short ride from the park's exit to a hospital."

Supported by Sam's body, mine bounced and rocked me into dreamland.

# Chapter Thirteen
## Sam

With my right ankle tightly wrapped in an elastic bandage and my right foot encased in a walking boot, I propped up my right leg on an opposite chair. I studied the few other people in the large waiting room. One woman was pacing. A man was wringing his hands together and staring into space. A couple sat in silence. At one point, the woman scooted closer to the man and rested her head on his shoulder.

Trying to divert my attention from the anxious individuals, my eyes glommed onto the wall clock. Following the second hand, I counted off the minutes until an hour passed.

As if they were thousands of worms, my nerves wriggled inside me. To shake off my growing tension, I wanted to stand and move about, but an incessant throbbing warned me to stay rooted to the plastic chair.

Through the lenses of my misty eyes, like an ominous cloud foretelling an upcoming storm, the doctor dressed in green scrubs seemed to roll toward me. Filled with trepidation, I implored the Lord to help Charley and her child.

Disregarding my aching ankle, I jumped up clinching my fists at my sides. "Is Charley alright?"

"Yes. She's fine."

I sucked in my breath, sighed, and turned my eyes upward and silently thanked God.

"But we couldn't save her baby."

Shamefully, I felt mixed emotions ranging from relief to a deep sadness. "Have you told her?"

"Yes, but in her groggy state, I'm not sure she grasped reality."

"Or she didn't want to."

She nodded. "I also assured her she'd be able to get pregnant again in the future."

"When can I see her?"

"In about three hours. She lost a great deal of blood, is sedated, and needs to sleep."

I shook her hand in appreciation. She turned and walked toward a set of double doors.

I returned to the row of seats and retrieved the crutches the nurse instructed me to use. Awkwardly, I shuffled to the cafeteria.

Despite being in a hospital, I was so hungry everything looked appealing. Unfortunately, after a few bites of the special—sliced turkey, smothered in gravy over mashed potatoes—I lost my appetite for the salty, greasy food. I even had difficulty forcing myself to eat the soggy unbuttered roll.

I left the space, went back to the waiting room, and did a bit of research on my smart phone. I called Child Protective Services and reported Charley's stepfather to an intake worker.

Although cordial, she wasn't reassuring. "While I appreciate your call, I'd prefer to speak to the victim, before filing a report."

I understood her position. My account was nothing more than hearsay.

To my surprise, I thought of calling Jack Nolan, the lawyer who worked in my building. The guy who'd asked me to lunch on several occasions. Anytime I'd seen him, he'd been impeccably dressed and exuded an air of confidence. I assumed he was as pushy and as arrogant as the partners in his firm were. At that moment, I thought those aggressive characteristics were exactly what Charley needed to convince the DA to accept her case.

My stomach lurched as an image of my stepdad flashed in my mind. Behind his professional exterior skulked a sinister man. He, too, wore expensive suits and imported shoes. In those days, he spent more money for a haircut then I presently did for my monthly car payment.

Hopefully, Jack wasn't all bad. Each time he'd asked me to lunch, I felt flattered. I couldn't deny his good looks tempted me. Like a teenager, butterflies fluttered in my stomach. In the next instant, angst wiped away by excitement and filled me with anger. Was it his habit to ask every woman in the building to lunch? Did he make the rounds? Was he just as phony as my stepdad hiding behind the guise of respectability? For all I knew he could be married and have half dozen children at home.

In response to his first lunch invitation I told him, "I'm too busy to socialize."

"Know the feeling," he replied. "Been working late nights and too many weekends since I got lucky enough to secure positions after law school. That's why I thought we could catch a quick bite together."

"I don't eat lunch." Not only was I rude my excuse was absurd.

"Call me if ever you'd like to. I'm usually stuck behind my desk and would always welcome the chance to come up for air."

*Sure. Right?* I thought.

Despite his recent banter with me on the elevator, I thought he'd be too preoccupied to speak to me. I was prepared to leave a brief summary of my reason for calling, but he cheerfully said, "Hi Sam. It's good to hear from you, but I thought you were on holiday."

Without hesitation, I bombarded him with details. As I did so, I realized it was foolish of me to think he'd accept Charley as a client. "Even if I could afford your rates, you probably wouldn't be interested in representing her. Perhaps, you might be able to give me a few referrals."

"Has she agreed to press charges?"

"I haven't asked her."

"Well if she does and the DA agrees to prosecute, I'll gladly represent her pro bono."

It surprised me Jack volunteered to take Charley's case. He seemed intent on rising up the corporate ladder of fame and fortune. In his polished demeanor, he didn't strike me as the type to risk his reputation to save a teenager, but maybe he needed a case like hers to improve his image. Egotistically, I wondered if he wanted to prove my first impression of him wrong. Regardless of his motivation, I was pleased to have found Charley a legitimate lawyer.

"When she's released from the hospital, can she come home with me?"

"Best speak to her before we start any legal action."

"Of course. I just know it isn't healthy for her to go back to her mother and stepdad."

He ignored my statement and asked, "Besides the victim's word, do you have any proof her stepfather raped her?"

"Like what?"

"DNA samples. Paternity tests are usually accurate after the eighth week of pregnancy."

"She was a traumatized frightened fifteen-year old. I doubt she sought prenatal care and even if she had I don't think she'd have requested an amniocentesis to prove her stepfather was her child's father."

"Maybe it's not too late to have DNA testing with tissue samples."

"After extensive hemorrhaging her child is gone." However, I gave Jack the name of Charley's physician. He promised to call her immediately after we spoke.

Knowing all I could do was wait I closed my eyes and rested.

# Chapter Fourteen
## Charley

When Sam entered the room, not wanting to hear what she had to say, I pretended to be sleeping.

Her lips tenderly brushed my cheek. Her fingertips smoothed my hair.

She whispered, "I'll be right here waiting for you to awake."

A peaceful feeling enveloped me. Soon, I drifted to a place I never wanted to leave.

*My arms gently rocked my babe. I sang her a lullaby. A great joy filled my heart.*

The dream turned into a nightmare.

*Why was she so silent, so still?*

*Longing to see my daughter's face, I unfolded the soft blanket, but she wasn't there.*

*Hot panic raced through me.*

*Where was she?*

*What monster had taken her from me?*

I screamed, "No, no. You can't have her."

My sweaty torso bolted straight up. Yanking a tube stuck in my arm, I felt a sharp pinch.

Surprising me, Sam tried to comfort me. "It's okay. You're safe now."

I stared into her warm eyes as she pressed my shoulders back.

My head nestled into the pillow.

She stroked my arms and pulled the sheet under my chin.

By then I remembered her coming close to my bed, but had no idea how long she'd been there.

"When you're stronger, would you like to come home with me? I don't think it wise for you to return to your mother's house. A lawyer named Jack Nolan will need your mother's legal consent for the hospital to release you to me."

I wasn't sure I understood her, until she said, "I'll leave his number by the phone. If you want to stay at my house ask your mother to call him."

"I want to be where my baby is. Take me to her."

Sam reached over the bed. Using a tissue, she wiped away my tears. "Charley, she's in Heaven with God."

"That's where I want to be, too. I need to be with her. Without her, I have nothing to live for."

# Chapter Fifteen
## Sam

The phone rang once, twice.

I asked, "Want me to answer it?"

Charley said, "I don't care."

I reached for the receiver. "Hi."

"Charley?"

"Just a moment, please." I gave the phone to Charley.

"Hello," she whispered.

Her pale face seemed to fade into the white pillowcase. "Hi, Mom."

To give her privacy, I slipped out of the room. I wondered if Charley would ask her mother for permission to stay with me.

In the waiting room, I tried calling Trudy hoping she was at the campground where there was a cell signal albeit a weak one.

She answered. "How's Charley doing?"

"As well as can be expected."

"What's that supposed to mean? Want to tell me what happened? The ranger only told us an ambulance took Charley to a hospital and you were with her. I passed the scanty information onto Charley's mother, who was beside herself with worry. She expressed appreciation for you staying at the hospital with Charley. She's out of town and wasn't sure when she'd be able to drive up here."

"Her mother just called and is speaking to Charley right now."

"I hope you get to meet her. She and her husband, Mike, are wonderful people. They're very active in our church always giving their time to help others."

Involuntarily I trembled. A part of me wanted to tell Trudy not to allow Mike anywhere near the young ladies at church, but I didn't dare betray Charley's confidence. Once she pressed charges against Mike, I trusted Trudy although shocked would make the appropriate decision to ensure he didn't interact with youth group members.

"I called to tell you I won't be coming back to camp." I not only didn't want to say too much about Charley's situation, I also felt that it was premature to tell Trudy about my plan to take Charley home with me. "Regardless of how long her stay, upon her release I'll make sure she gets to Stockton safely. Can you pack up our gear and take it home with you? When you get back to the office on Monday, I'll need you to cancel my appointments for the week."

"Of course, but why?"

"I hurt my ankle and think it best to work from home for a few days."

"Is it a serious injury?"

"No. It's nothing really, but I'm going to follow doctor's orders and stay off it for a while."

Without asking any other questions she offered, "I'll do whatever I can to help. Although I can tell you don't want to tell me what's really going on, I want to thank you for being there for Charley. You turned out to be one heck of an extraordinary chaperone."

"Thanks, Trudy."

Five minutes later, I peeked into Charley's room. The phone was back in its cradle and Charley once again was asleep.

A few hours later, she awakened.

"Hi," I whispered.

She continued to stare into space.

I wheeled a tray in front of her. "Want something to eat."

She pushed it to the side.

Her glassy eyes frightened me.

A nurse came into the room and asked Charley why she hadn't touched her meal.

Charley didn't respond.

Next, her doctor approached. She nodded to me and greeted Charley. "I have a list of questions to ask you."

I stepped away from the bed out of earshot. The doctor drew the curtain halfway.

Standing outside the open door, I saw Charley moving her head up and down or from side to side.

When the doctor stepped into the corridor, I whispered, "I'm worried about Charley. She seems dazed. Is she going to be okay?"

"Her response is typical of someone under the influence of sedating drugs. Once they wear off she'll be alert."

Holding on to hope, I tried to dismiss my fears of Charley sinking into a deep depression,

At eight-thirty when a nurse recommended I leave for the night, I told Charley. "My cell number is next to the phone. Call me at any hour if you want to talk. I'll be back early in the morning."

She acknowledged me with a slight nod.

Before leaving the hospital, I passed a gift shop and glanced into the storefront window.

A salesperson must have thought I was a perspective shopper. She promptly held open the door. "See something you like? We're having a sale on summer items."

"Do you have women's clothes?"

"Being so many tourists end up needing the hospital we carry things to make their stay in our little town comfortable."

While paying for two sundresses, undergarments, a pair of pajamas, sandals, and some toiletries I asked the friendly woman, "Is there a hotel nearby?"

"Our one and only motel is right across the street. I'll gladly escort you there."

Despite me trying to assure her, I could make the trip on my own, she insisted on carrying my bags. She waited for me to register and walked me to my room. I offered to give her something for her time, but she refused. "All part of my shop's service."

Feeling grungy still dressed in yesterday's outfit and after the day's ordeal, I took a hot shower.

Before being completely dry, my phone rang.

Glancing at the caller ID I saw Jack's name. "Hi," I said.

He explained the reason for his call, "I spoke to Charley's mother. She gave her consent for you to have temporary custody of her daughter."

"Wonderful. Maybe her mother is more protective than I thought."

"That was the good news. The bad news is Charley won't be pressing charges against Mike. Her mother claimed Mike is innocent. Charley made up the story because she didn't want her mother to know about her promiscuous behaviors."

"Can't say I'm surprised by her mother's statement."

"With your permission, I'd like to speak to Charley in person. I'd like to hear what she wants to do directly from her."

"It's fine with me. I can bring her to your office after we're back in Stockton."

"I'd like to visit her tomorrow while she's still in the hospital."

"It's a long drive."

"I have no weekend plans. Besides I'd like to hand deliver the original legal document awarding you temporary guardianship of Charley."

"How did you get a judge to sign it so quickly especially on a Friday?"

"I have my ways."

I wondered, *Of working magic or working the system.*

# Chapter Sixteen
## Charley

After telling Mom the truth about Mike and my miscarriage, her jabs as sharp as the edge of a razorblade slashed my broken heart. I tried not to pay much attention to what she said, but since she hung up her words keep spinning like a top round and round in my mind.

"Whatever you did I forgive you, but there's no need to drag Mike's good name into your sordid life.

"It isn't important who the boy was. As long as you promise never to see him again, we don't need to know his name. After all, it's your fault he deflowered you. You're the Jezebel who seduced him. You're the girl who sinned."

"Mom, I can't come home. I can't face..." Mike's name stuck in my throat. *Why didn't she believe me? Why was she protecting him?*

"God spared you the embarrassment of a full term pregnancy of you wearing your shame for the entire congregation to see. I'll protect you and see to it no one ever knows what you did. If you learn from your mistake, you can have a happy future and marry a respectable man like your dad, Mike. The proof of his worth is he's forgiven you and says he bears no malice toward you regardless of what you've done."

"The lady from church, the chaperone, Sam, offered me a place to stay."

"Remember it's your family, Mike and I, who will stick by you and faithfully keep your secret. Don't be telling some stranger your outlandish delusions."

I dared not mention my conversations with Sam. I dared not tell her Sam probably reported Mike to Child Protective Services.

Mom kept talking, "Your dad and I are rekindling our romance and it might be better for you to stay away for a while just until you recuperate and get those crazy ideas of insulting Mike out of your head. I wouldn't want to upset him with your nonsense. I wouldn't want you to anger him."

"Then I can go home with Sam?"

"Yes you can. That is as long as you swear to me on the Holy Bible you won't destroy my marriage by doing anything foolish."

"Like what?"

"Like telling Sam or your doctor or the authorities lies about Mike. Will you promise me to keep your fanciful accusations to yourself?"

"You mean you don't want me to press charges against Mike for raping me?"

"Exactly!"

"Without my baby to protect I don't care about him anymore."

"The matter's settled. You go stay with Sam. I'll forgive you for making up nasty stories and we'll all forget about these few days of your life. Soon it'll feel like it never happened."

But she was wrong. I would never forget my baby. I would never stop missing her. I wanted to go to her, but I knew if I took my own life, God would send me straight to hell.

If Sam really wanted to help me, she'd figure out a way for me to leave this earth and be with my child.

Nah. She'd never do that.

Even in the bright sunlight, my world was dark.

Without my daughter, I was all alone with a dirty past and my only prospects were of a nasty future.

# Chapter Seventeen
## Sam

The sound of my cell phone ringing drew me out of a deep sleep.

Jack's name flashed on my screen. I guessed he changed his mind about making the three-hour drive to see Charley. Truthfully, I couldn't blame him.

"Hi. Don't worry. I can understand you not wanting to drive all the way out here."

Without fanfare he instructed, "I need you to go on Facebook and cancel Charley's page. There're photos of her in comprised positions. She seems to be advertising for a guy, maybe a pimp, to take care of her."

"What are you saying? How can I access her account?"

"As her legal guardian, you can report the page. She claims to be nineteen. To prove otherwise, I've emailed an attachment of her birth certificate along with a copy of the court order naming you her legal custodian.

"Do it before her classmates see the page. It's only been up for a few days and she already has lots of likes from scores of men."

"Charley couldn't have done this. She hasn't had access to a computer since she left home."

"The post went up early Thursday morning, before she left for the camping trip."

"Why would she do that if she was planning to run away? Mike probably set up the Facebook page from his PC and photoshopped the pictures. He may've only allowed her access to it to do her schoolwork. Maybe he added the page to warn her he'd destroy her if she told anyone about what he'd done."

I heard Jack exhaling a deep breath. "No matter the why, just follow the directions I sent you and the page will no longer exist. I'll see you at the hospital in a few hours."

With a new rush of anger seething inside me, following the steps outlined in Jack's email, I was able to have Charley's fictitious page removed from social media.

I knelt down next to the bed and thanked God Jack's diligence averted Mike's attempt at assaulting Charley yet another time.

In the shower, knowing that dwelling on Mike's transgressions wouldn't help me comfort Charley I tried to rinse away my rage.

With each bite of breakfast, I felt renewed energy, which I hoped I could somehow transmit to Charley.

Wanting to thank the shopkeeper for her kindness, I stopped by the gift shop. While I was there I purchased a crocheted shawl.

Minutes later, I stepped into Charley's room and peeked behind the drawn curtain. She was alone staring into space.

"How you feeling?" I asked.

She grunted. "Like I could sleep forever."

"Want to talk?"

"Not really."

I glanced at the untouched tray. "Don't like hospital food?"

"I'm not hungry."

"You'll need to eat and gain strength if you want your doctor to release you tomorrow."

"Looking at this is making me sick." Charley pushed the cart causing the dishes to rattle and the apple juice to splash her nightgown and sheets.

"Do you want me to call a nurse to help you shower?"

"No," Charley shouted. She dashed from the bed into the adjoining bathroom.

An orderly changed the bed. She knocked on the bathroom door. "I'll leave a clean nightgown on the doorknob.

Charley opened the door and snatched the printed garment.

Sitting quietly listening to the sound of the shower, I hoped Charley would emerge refreshed.

With a towel wrapped around her hair, she settled back in bed.

I told her, "The attorney I mentioned, Jack Nolan, will be stopping by today. He has a good track record as a defense lawyer."

"So?"

"He's willing to represent you free of charge."

"I don't need an attorney. I'm not going to press charges against Mike."

"Why not?"

Charley shrugged her shoulders.

"Don't you think he should be punished for what he did?"

"Yea, but he won't be. Like my mom, the church people, and everyone else will believe his word against mine."

"Don't you want to stop him from hurting someone else?"

"Sure, but like I said I don't have the power to stop him. And don't call Child Protective Services. If anyone of their people talks to me, I'll deny the story I told you." She closed her eyes shutting me out for the next several hours.

As if she had removed her warmth, the room became chilled. I stretched out my legs on a chair and draped the shawl over them. I tried reading a science fiction novel. Usually by losing myself into futuristic worlds, I escaped reality, but today I had difficulty concentrating.

This situation felt daunting. Unlike a challenging work assignment, I didn't have resources to locate answers. I didn't have any prior cases to draw from.

I desperately wanted to reach Charley, make a difference in her life, and help her to move forward. But how could I when I, too, was stuck in the past?

Thoughts drifted to my teen years when without a supportive mother I needed someone else to rescue me. Lucky for me my father believed me. But he chose not to be a big part of my life. He continued living in Japan and his calls became less frequent. Last time I saw him was five years ago.

To Charley I was a stranger, someone she didn't know. If she couldn't trust her own mother, how could she trust me?

I studied the hospital room's soothing bisque colored walls. Striped drapes flanked the windows. Yet these accents did little to remove the austere ambiance. It reminded me of the boarding school I'd attended. Faculty members wore smiles like lipstick painted on their faces. I didn't feel they genuinely welcomed me or cared about me.

Did Charley feel the same way about the nurses, doctors, and me?

I peered out the window to the mountain backdrop. Being far from home felt strange. I seldom ventured from Stockton not because I was especially fond of the city, but because it was familiar. When I went to boarding school, despite feeling relief to be away from my wicked stepfather I missed my room, my things.

Would Charley feel the same way about being at my house? Would she still feel frightened, just as I felt every day of my life since my evil stepfather taught me the world wasn't a safe place?

A knock on Charley's hospital room door announced Jack's arrival.

He acknowledged me with a wink.

Dressed in faded jeans, a knit shirt, and a worn pair of loafers he looked exceedingly handsome. I felt an uncommon tingling beginning in my stomach and spreading to my toes and fingertips. I dispelled the schoolgirl crush by admonishing myself. Jack was here on business not to court me. Besides, the last thing I wanted was a romantic relationship.

His kind gesture of bringing a bouquet of daisies for Charley made me smile.

He tiptoed toward the bed. Charley appeared to be sleeping, but she opened her eyes when he placed the vase on her nightstand.

He said. "Good afternoon. I'm Jack, Sam's friend."

"I don't need a lawyer."

"But you need a ride to Sam's place and so does she."

She frowned.

"Want to take the scenic route home?"

"I don't care."

I joined the conversation, "If you feel up to it, maybe we can stop somewhere along the way for a bite to eat. Anything's got to better than hospital food."

"Sounds like a plan," Jack said.

Charley firmly ordered, "Can you two just leave? I'm tired and want to sleep."

Jack responded, "Good idea. Sam and I'll go have an early dinner. Can we bring you something?"

"Nah. I don't have much of an appetite, but I'm really tired. Do me a favor and don't come back."

Respecting Charley's wish I said, "See you in the morning."

# Chapter Eighteen
## Charley

I heard an orderly say, "Your evening meal is mac'n'cheese. If you're anything like my teenage daughter you won't be able to resist."

I waited until I heard her shuffle out of the room before opening my eyes.

Although sounding tempting, one sniff of the so-called comfort food triggered lonely memories. When Mom was stuck at work or out to dinner with some guy, left to fend for myself I prepared boxes of the stuff and each time it felt satisfying to eat every bit of it at least for a few minutes.

Thinking of how often she left me on my own made me mad.

What really got me was her choice to ignore the truth about Mike. He was just plain evil. How could she let him be alone with me?

But then again, she made excuses for him mistreating and disrespecting her.

How could I expect her to stop him from hurting me when she didn't even protect herself from his wicked ways?

I was sure she had to know he was bad through and through. Did she think so little of herself so little of me to let him get away with yelling, insulting, and pushing us around? With all the bad things he'd done to her—squandering her money, using her, and belittling her not to mention how he treated me with contempt—how could she choose to stick up for him?

Mom was a light sleeper. There wasn't any way she didn't know the truth about Mike coming to my room during the night. The thought of her in bed knowing what he was up to repulsed me.

What kind of person wouldn't stop a rapist?

What kind of a mother was she?

I threw my fork across the room. It made a sharp clanking noise as it hit the polished floor.

"What was the point of living?" I screamed.

Mike had won. No one would believe he had violated me. He'd destroyed my reputation.

I turned my eyes upward. "God, are you on Mike's side, too? Is that why You took away my baby my only hope for happiness?

"If You keep me alive, I swear I'll no longer play by Your holy rules.

"To get even with You, I'll start sleeping with every guy I meet."

Why shouldn't I be a tramp? I have nothing to lose, no friends to alienate, no loving mother to disgrace, no father to embarrass, no God to offend.

Probably all the kids I know had already heard about me being knocked up. They're probably spreading lies about me on Facebook. Good thing I never had a page of my own. And I didn't visit their sites because I never wanted to hear them bragging about the good times they shared. And for sure, I don't want to know what stories they're spreading about me.

I never fit in before and now they had new reasons to shun me.

I'd live up to my ugly image.

I'd be the trashy girl they thought I was.

After all, I was just a used discarded object anyone could kick around in the mud.

# Chapter Nineteen
## Sam

While Jack politely held the door open for me, leaning on my crutches I awkwardly made my way out of Charley's room.

As we walked through the brightly lit corridor, guilt washed over me. "I feel awful about you driving all this way when it's doubtful Charley will agree to press charges against Mike."

"Maybe it'll be for the best if she doesn't."

I wondered if he was backing out of his word to defend her. "What are you saying?"

"Her story will be out there for everyone to hear. People, especially teens, can be insensitive. Whatever the outcome she'll get deeply hurt during the process."

"You mean even if she wins she'll lose?"

"Something like that. And at this point I'm not sure the DA will take her case. From the little research I did, I found out Mike has a stellar reputation in the community and is respected at his church."

"All the more reason to stop his charade."

"If only it were a just world I'd agree with you, but the reality is he has a better chance of coming out of this like a hero than a villain." Jack abruptly changed the subject. "What type of food would you like? Want to stay in town or are you up for a drive?"

"What's your preference?"

By then, we'd reached the hospital's entrance.

"You wait right here while I get my car."

While I waited, I tried to put myself in Charley's place. Sure I would've wanted my stepdad exposed, but at what cost?

Sure, I would've wanted to shield my mom. I wouldn't have wanted our family and her friends to have known how she failed to protect me. I wouldn't have wanted anyone to think less of her.

But, I wondered, was that because I loved her or was it because her choosing my stepdad over me meant I was a worthless daughter? Would I have wanted everyone to know I was an unimportant person?

In the end, was I thinking of her or of me?

Jack's husky voice brought me back to the present. "I'll help you get into the car," he offered as he reached for my crutches.

Wanting to keep our interactions strictly business and wanting to focus on Charley, I didn't want him to fuss over me. "It's only a sprained ankle. I think the crutches and this silly walking boot are overkill." I handed him my crutches and slid onto the passenger seat.

As he pulled away from the curb, he responded. "Sometimes it's a good thing to slow down and take it easy."

"Strange advice coming from a man like you. Bet you're a high energy workaholic who toils into the wee hours even on weekends and postpones vacations."

"Maybe so, but I've learned I do my best work when there's balance in my life."

"Like what?"

"Like spending time with friends, taking walks, and planting flowers in my garden."

"I can see why you're a trial lawyer."

"You think I'm all talk."

"Sorry I didn't mean to offend you."

"I'm glad you feel comfortable enough to share your honest thoughts."

Strangely, I did feel comfortable talking with him even though he was a man.

He continued, "You're right about me being a workaholic, but I'm trying not to be obsessive. For example, unless I have a court date looming, I take weekends off."

"What are you doing here this weekend?"

"Enjoying your company."

Attempting to push away his compliment, I changed the subject.

"Were you surprised about Charley's mom giving me temporary custody?"

"Not really. I think not having to relate to Charley right now might be easier for her than having to confront Mike, a man I think she fears."

"Have you had similar cases in the past?"

"I've had my share of situations involving dysfunctional families."

"Have they depressed you?"

"A bit, but mostly they've helped me appreciate my own childhood all the more. While I was growing up, I felt my mom fussed too much and my dad worked too much."

As he spoke, I envisioned Jack as a cute mischievous kid.

"I loved the hours I spent with my dad working on his treasured antique car. He was patient, seldom lost his temper, and taught me to be independent."

"Sounds like you have a wise father."

"Yea, my dad's a great guy. My mom's pretty nice, too."

He glanced over at me, "What about you? What was your childhood like?"

I swallowed back waves of sadness. I turned away hoping I wouldn't drown in a rush of tears.

"I'm sorry," he said. "That's none of my business."

I stared out the window. The sky exploded with vibrant colors. Rather than one dominating over another, reds, pinks, and purples kept their identities yet blended without a beginning or end to form a magnificent panorama. The majesty of the setting sun seemed to symbolize an ideal family where individualism could shine in a bright circle of love.

# Chapter Twenty
## Charley

I liked the way Jack talked to me not down to me. I felt a good vibe from him.

But I didn't want to be a gullible fool like Mom.

I hoped the way he held the door for Sam wasn't part of his lawyer's act. When they were standing side by side, I thought they made a nice looking couple. She was so pretty with a button nose, full lips, and shiny curly chestnut hair resting on the shoulders of her slim petite body. And he could be a TV soap opera star with his sandy straight hair falling on his forehead above his very cute face.

I hoped they really were decent people. I hoped they genuinely treated each other with respect.

I wanted to trust my gut. I wanted to believe I could see people for who they really were.

When I first saw Sam, I sensed her loneliness. I felt bad for my annoyance at her attempts at being friendly. I felt I was hurting her feelings by shutting her out. Maybe if I'd met her at another time, I would've trusted her at least a little bit.

I thought of the first time Mom introduced me to Mike. He used sweet words, but I could tell he was holding down an ugly rage. I cringed when he grabbed my arm and squeezed it a little too hard as if to let me know he was boss. And boss he was of my mom, the house, and for too long of me.

Jack didn't seem like know it all Mike. But, maybe Jack was showing his professional side. Maybe he was better at hiding his flaws. If Jack were better at fooling folks, he'd be more dangerous than Mike.

I watched Mike in church convincing the congregation he was a devout man. I watched him in restaurants pretending to be some rich guy. He'd make flowery comments to young waitresses as he ogled their cleavages. My mom didn't want to notice, but it was obvious if given the chance Mike would hook up with every woman on the planet. He was a slimeball. I just couldn't believe why I was the only one who could see through his thin dishonest skin.

Thinking of Mike rekindled my desire to be strong. He'd taught me it was best not to trust anyone in this sick, sick world.

If I had to go on living, I'd have to make it on my own without a Sam or a Jack to help me.

It was too late.

No one, not even God, could undo the past.

No one except God could give me back my baby, but I knew he wouldn't.

# Chapter Twenty-One
## Sam

After studying the legal document awarding me temporary custody of Charley, her physician released the teen into my care.

With the aid of crutches, I walked at Charley's side as a nurse wheeled her through the hospital's double doors.

At the sight of Jack leaning against his BMW, I felt an unfamiliar elation.

He quickly came to attention and greeted us with a wave. In the next moment, he opened the front passenger door and extended a hand to Charley.

She pushed his hand aside, raised herself up, and transferred seats.

He took my crutches and stowed the aluminum pair in his trunk.

Once in the back of his car, I relaxed by stretching my legs across the cool gray leather.

The nurse fastened Charley's seatbelt and said, "Nice car."

Charley didn't seem to notice.

"Sure is," I said.

Once we were on the road, Jack asked, "In a few weeks, why don't the three of us return to check out Rainbow Falls?"

"I'd love to see them," I said.

Charley didn't comment.

"Have you been there before?" I asked him.

"Nope."

Remembering last night's conversation I teased. "Been too busy?"

"Guess I could use that as an excuse, but truth be told I'd forgotten how magical the forest could be until I inhaled the glorious clean air."

I thought of Friday trudging my injured leg through the twisting trail, sweating, and in pain. Maybe I was too afraid of not finding Charley to notice the ambiance or maybe I was just insensitive to nature's beauty.

Jack interrupted the tiresome images parading in my mind. "Having grown up in New York City I didn't get to see many trees. I was ten when my parents sent me to summer camp for the first time. Enjoying horsing around with other kids, I didn't appreciate my surroundings. Like most boys, I was interested in hiking, climbing, and constantly looking forward to my next meal. My counselor, filled with wisdom, had an old soul housed in his young body. One day he asked us to look at tops of the pine trees."

As if on cue I craned my neck, looked out the window, and followed a line of tall pines.

Jack continued talking. "He pointed out each crown had its own space. None touched another."

Instead of being a green blur, I focused on each pine tree noticing the phenomenon he'd described.

"The counselor explained as part of the same family, pines give each other space for their crowns to each have a place in the sun. At first, I didn't get his analogy. Maybe the other kids didn't either because he said, 'Too bad human families can't give all their members the respect they deserve.'"

I twisted my body in order to see part of Charley's face. A tear slid down her cheek. Obviously, his story hit home. I swallowed back sadness thinking of my parents too involved in their own dramas to have been interested in my life, my hopes, my dreams.

Jack's story made me question why I'd stereotyped him as a slick, glib lawyer. Was he just pretending to have a positive side or was he genuinely a good person?

# Chapter Twenty-Two
## Charley

Not interested in the sights, I closed my eyes.

If Sam and Jack thought I was asleep, I hoped they wouldn't say things I'd rather not hear.

I thought of the awful things I'd overheard between Mom and Mike. He'd spout empty promises and she'd gush with words of undying love. Even when we were driving to church, he'd sometimes coax her to talk dirty. He said it turned him on.

Yuck. He was a loudmouth slob. Many a night I fell asleep with ear buds stuck in my ears listening to blasting music.

Whenever possible I chose not to be in the same room with them together. There was no avoiding his cheap talk when Mom and I prepared meals exactly to his rigid specifications. If we left out or added an ingredient, he'd get real mad. He'd use his arm to push his plate off the table. The dish would break into pieces. Food would be everywhere and he'd say, "See what you made me do. Clean up this mess and make me something edible."

The guy was obsessive about the house being clean and perfectly neat. Nothing could be out of place. No cobwebs could hide in any corner. Yet, he never hesitated to make messes. Anytime we didn't pour his coffee he made a point to spill some on the counter or leave a ring on the furniture. He repeatedly told us we could've avoided the extra work of cleaning up after him if we'd just served him from the start.

After he showered, he threw his wet towels on the floor. As if he were in a hotel he expected Mom or I to be his personal maids to replace them with fluffy fresh ones.

Truth was we were steps lower than servants. We were battered slaves.

After he broke things, we had to repair or replace the objects with Mom's money of course.

The best times were when he went out alone especially at night. Mom and I were together, which felt nice until she'd tell me how she worried about him and hoped he wouldn't get in an accident.

Didn't she know he was cheating on her?

Sam and Jack didn't talk much making me wonder if they weren't a couple after all.

# Chapter Twenty-Three
## Sam

Trying not to disturb Charley as she slept, I avoided conversing with Jack.

"Want to stop to eat?" he asked.

"No. I think it best if she sleeps. Let's go straight to my place."

Once again, my mind drifted to the past.

Why had I forgotten the extent of my stepfather's violation? Why didn't I realize when I wasn't able to be in the same room with him that what he'd done to me was more than an attempt at fondling me? He didn't merely touch me over my pajamas. He didn't just laugh at me. He didn't just threaten to undress me. He raped me.

I now understood why I cringed whenever I heard the words date rape. The term reduced actual rape to the lowest common denominator. The intensity of rape and date rape were as different as the intensity of a severe storm and the magnitude of a category four hurricane.

A man taking advantage of an inebriated woman was indeed a despicable act, but it wasn't on the same level as a powerful threatening man viciously hurting an innocent victim.

Rape wasn't a crime of lust. It was a crime of violence.

Why hadn't it dawned on me, the reason I still couldn't say my stepfather's name was because he didn't just frighten me, make a pass at me, or acted inappropriately. Fact was he violated me. No wonder I viewed him as a revolting monster.

By shoving horrific memories deep inside, was I like the proverbial secret skeleton hiding in a closet? Was that why I didn't date and hardly socialized? Had I traded remembering the truth for something almost as bad, isolation?

When Jack approached Stockton exits, he asked, "Are we getting close?"

Switching to the moment, I shut off my thoughts and directed him to my condo.

Within minutes, when we arrived at my house I said, "I'll unlock the garage door and manually open it."

He suggested, "Please give me your keys. I'll get the door. You need to stay off that foot as much as possible."

Although it wasn't necessary, I thought it considerate of him.

He unlocked the outside lock and lifted the garage door to an empty bay.

I told him, "She'll be staying on the lower level."

He pulled into the garage. "If you'd like, tomorrow I'll ask a friend for a ride so I can drive your car back from the church's parking lot."

"Thank you. That would be nice."

Careful not to startle her I gently nudged Charley's shoulder. "We've arrived."

She slowly exited the car.

It was my habit not to wear shoes at home. There was something homey about walking around barefoot. Unconsciously I slipped off my sandal, but didn't remove the walking boot. Having the clumsy footwear to mobilize my ankle made walking awkward. Without the crutches, it was difficult to keep my balance.

I opened the garage's side door to the ground level. Diffused sunlight from a transom cast an abstract pattern on the walls.

As usual, the hardwood floor felt warm and cozy.

Charley followed me through the foyer into the guest room.

Jack trailed behind us with my crutches.

I asked Charley, "Can I fix you something to eat?"

"I'm not hungry."

"I don't have much food in the house. Want to go grocery shopping to pick out your favorites?"

"I don't want to go anywhere."

She stood a few feet from me, but it felt as if she were miles away.

Jack said, "I'll go get some burgers. What kind of shakes would you two like?"

"I'll have strawberry," I said, but Charley didn't express a preference.

In the brightness drifting in from the guestroom's small oval window, I felt a bit embarrassed about the room's shabby appearance. It still had the bedroom set and dated bedding I'd inherited from the previous owners. Knowing my mom wouldn't want to visit without her husband and me refusing to allow him to stay under my roof I didn't bother to invest time or money into improving the space. Clinging to the hope my mom would surprise me with her presence I left the room untouched figuring she'd want to pick out things she liked in order to make the room her own.

"Sorry for the Spartan ambiance." Rather than admitting no one had ever stayed overnight I fibbed, "I seldom have reason to use this space. I'll throw these sheets in the wash."

Charley came over to help, but Jack said, "I can do that." He gathered the linens in his arms. "Where's your machine?"

"The laundry room is up two flights between my office and my bedroom."

Before leaving the guestroom he said, "I'll start the wash then go get lunch."

I turned to Charley. "Sorry the bed's not ready. Want to lie down in my room?"

"I'm not tired," she said and sat on the bare mattress.

"While you're here, this'll be your room. You can decorate it to your liking. It'll be fun going shopping for fresh bedding, pictures, but first these walls need a pop of color. "

Again, Charley didn't respond.

Looking at her vacant eyes, I feared she was too depressed to be in the house alone and decided I'd give Trudy a call Monday morning advising her I'd be working remotely for a longer time. She could email me materials I'd need to complete the cases I was working on and I could occasionally stop by the office to attend meetings with clients.

"Have you spoken with your mother today? Does she know you've been discharged from the hospital?" I asked.

Charley shook her head.

Placing my cell on the night table, I jotted my address on a notepad. "Use my cell to call your mother. She's welcome to visit."

Charley didn't make an effort to move.

I remembered my first day at boarding school. After arriving in my room, I sat on my designated twin bed and stared out the window, but as if a fog covered my sight, I didn't see anything. A part of me thought if I stayed absolutely still I'd blend into the austere decor and be invisible.

A high-pitched bell sounded announcing lunch, but I didn't stir. I hoped in an institution full of strangers no one would notice I was missing.

I ignored a faint knock on the door.

A cheery voice said, "Hi. I'm Beth your roomy." She sat next to me. "When I first arrived I cried for days. I couldn't stop thinking about the life I once lived. Mom and Dad were terrific. They showered me with attention. I was so happy in our pretty house. After my parents' fatal accident, I was angry with God for taking them away from me.

"I lived with my aunt. I did anything and everything I could think of to get into trouble. I disobeyed her rules, made terrible messes, sassed her, stole from her, and stayed out nights hiding in sordid places.

"My aunt thought I was acting too crazy for her to handle having me around. In desperation, she sent me here.

"Didn't she know she was ripping me away from all things familiar, my school, my friends, and my cat? Not admitting I drove her to the point of getting rid of me, I thought she was the cruelest person I'd ever met.

"It took a long while, but I finally got used to being here. Much later, I realized there was a reason, although I had no clue what it could be, that the tragedy happened. Once I accepted things as they were, I noticed life wasn't so bad."

Her story, so much worse than mine, made me ashamed of feeling sorry for myself.

She offered, "Stick with me and I'll show you the upside of this place."

She taught me the ropes and protected me from the mean girls. Most of all she was fun. She often said, "Where else could you have a sleepover every night with your bestie?"

After we graduated and went to different colleges, at first, I missed her so much and wrote often, but her responses were brief notes months apart. She encouraged me to make new friends and she urged me to date. She said being in a coed dorm was the best part of college. I, on the other hand, had no interest in getting to know guys. I buried myself in books. Intent on being an 'A' student I deliberately avoided the social scene.

Gradually, Beth and I lost touch.

I often wondered what she was up to, where she was living. I wondered why I'd let her disappear from my life.

I would never forget her kindness.

I only hoped I could be a Beth for Charley.

# Chapter Twenty-Four
## Charley

In the strange room staring at a blank white wall, I wondered if I should just walk out the door and try my luck living on the street. But why should I make an effort to do anything? As long as no one bothered me, I could hide from the world in Sam's house.

Not that it mattered, but I couldn't believe she'd actually let me make personal changes to her condo. When she suggested I could help her redecorate, I thought she was only trying to impress Jack until I realized he'd already left the room.

In my mom's house, I had no say in what color walls were painted or which pieces of furniture went where. Everything about our place was decided by Mike. He dictated the placement of all objects from the biggest to the smallest. He was obsessive about everything having a place and everything always being in its place. He went beyond neatness.

Most pieces of furniture were only for show. Like the living room end tables. No magazines, glasses, or anything could rest on their highly polished surfaces.

Before using the bathroom in the morning, I had to make up my bed. Mike didn't allow me to leave any personal items on my desk. I could only use it to do homework. As soon as I completed my assignments, I had to put my books in my backpack and place it on the top shelf of my bookcase until I took it to school.

No matter how much my mom raved about his good taste, because the house was all about him, I hated the place and thought it was ugly.

Before Mike arrived, I loved hanging out in my tiny room. One of Mike's first official acts was to destroy my treasures. He ripped a poster off the wall next to my bed. He slit the few stuffed animals I'd won at the fair before shoving them into a black plastic bag. He smashed my snow globe against the door. The glass shattered and white flakes came pouring down. They reminded me of the frozen tears locked behind my eyes.

Once we moved into his house, he put me in a room at the end of a long hallway. He warned me not to change anything or add anything. It had a bed covered with a drab quilt, a small dresser, a desk, an office chair, and a clothes closet. I didn't have a cell phone or my own computer. I had to ask him permission to use his.

Like some kind of a drill sergeant, he'd come around inspecting my room. "You have to learn to keep this space shipshape," he'd shout.

He tried to control my life.

He frowned upon me reading secular books. "You should be reading and rereading the Bible," he roared. "How else are you going to learn to be obedient?"

When I complained to Mom, she said, "If it weren't for Mike we'd still be living in that cramped apartment. You'd still be sleeping in a room no bigger than your new closet."

Guess she was right about some things. I remembered at our last place the awful days of being in her way when she entertained her men friends. She'd scoot me out of the living room where the TV was. She didn't allow me to go to the kitchen for snacks. Only in an emergency could I use the bathroom, because she might decide to shower with one of her lovers. I had to stay as quiet as a mouse.

The memories made me shiver. She was always trying to please some loser: a drunk, a drug addict or a mean no good rotten louse. I couldn't remember a time when she thought of me before some guy.

Hating to listen to the lies she and Mike told each other or hear the disgusting sounds of them having sex, I crawled in a corner, covered my ears, and wished I could dissolve into nothingness.

Mom worshiped the ground Mike walked on. From out of nowhere, he came to the neighborhood to stay with an elderly lady from our church. The woman didn't have family and he offered to help her with chores and the like. When she died, she left him her house. It was a three-bedroom in the best part of town. I always suspected he conned her into changing her will. Once she'd done what he wanted, I think he did some awful something to rush her death. By then he was a deacon in our church and no one else doubted he was a caring, selfless man and deserved the generous inheritance.

Mom was crazy with happiness when he proposed. She danced around the apartment singing. She thought of Mike as her prince charming. She was delighted to move into his big house and said the least we could do was to keep it immaculate for Mr. Big Shot Mike, the most important person in her life.

Thinking of Mom prompted me to give her a call.

"Honey," she screeched. "I just stepped in the door. We got home late last night after a blissful couple of days at the lake. Even though he must be exhausted, Mike is still at church mingling with parishioners."

I knew their Sunday routine. He'd socialize while she worked for hours fixing him an elegant dinner.

She rambled, "I'm so excited. We're going on a trip far away."

I wondered what it would cost her to take him somewhere that special.

"Mike's been just wonderful trying to console me about your..." she trailed off.

Her alluding to the fact I'd lost my baby made me feel woozy.

"Even though he doesn't deserve your horrid accusations, he's not angry at you. He says when you're ready he'll be there for you."

Images of Mike naked and coming toward me made be nauseous. Just in case I had to throw up, I carried the phone into the adjoining bathroom, sat on the cold tile floor and lifted the toilet seat.

I needed to figure out a way never to see him again, but knew he'd come after me, force himself on me again and again.

To stop the terrible images swirling in my mind I forced myself to listen to Mom. She kept bragging about Mike. No matter how much he used her, she still didn't get it. The man she claimed to love should be in a jail cell for life. Just goes to show, she didn't know anything about love.

"You still there?" she asked.

I swallowed an urge to scream at her by saying. "Yea Mom. I gotta go. Just wanted to tell you I'm back in town."

Preoccupied with pleasing Mike she wouldn't dream of visiting me.

Fearing Mike, I purposely didn't encourage her or give her Sam's address.

"Good thing the church lady let you stay with her. I have lots to do to get ready including working a few extra shifts to make us some spending money for our future travels. Let's get together when Mike and I come back from our second honeymoon."

"Sure, Mom." I hoped my voice didn't sound as disappointed as I felt.

"Bye, baby girl."

The phone went dead.

I buried my face in the bare mattress hoping to stifle my sobs.

Why did I expect her to behave differently?

Why?

Because like Mom, I was a ridiculous fool.

# Chapter Twenty-Five
## Sam

Following doctor's orders, I'd only taken showers in the motel. Looking forward to a soothing soak, I removed the walking boot and unwound the restricting compression bandage. On this hot day, I languished in a tub of tepid water fragrant with herbal bath salts. Soon, a throbbing in my lower leg made me realize I needed to rewrap my injury, fast and tight.

Hobbling in my room, I found myself having difficulty deciding what to wear. I didn't want Charley to think I was too conservative or too old to be her friend.

I also had to admit I wanted Jack to find me attractive. The thought of him made my cheeks burn. At the same time, I felt an anxious knot twist in my stomach.

I admonished myself for having the erratic feelings.

Since Charley wasn't going to press charges against Mike, she didn't need a lawyer. My guess was Jack and I would merely go back to occasionally seeing each other in our office building.

Wanting to dress more like a teenager, I slipped on a jeans skirt and a tank top. I'd purchased both items the night before the camping trip. While packing I doubted my choices thinking the skirt was impractical and the top was too risqué for a chaperone to wear. After seeing the abbreviated outfits the teens and adults were wearing, I realized this outfit would've fit right in.

I stared in the mirror surprised to see patches of peeling skin, guessing the other day's exposure to too much sun did some damage. I attempted to cover up the flakes by applying makeup, but couldn't hide a line of freckles across my nose.

I laughed. The freckles reminded me of a vacation I'd spent with my parents at the beach. My father teased. "Your teacher won't have to ask how you spent your weekend. One look at your freckled face will announce the hours you frolicked in the sun."

He was right about the fond memories I had of us being together for the last time before he left for Japan.

As my hair dried, curls sprang up in all directions. I thought of straightening it with a flat iron but a chirp from the washing machine prompted me to head to the laundry room to switch Charley's sheets from the washer to the dryer.

Without the aid of crutches, I felt irritating sharp pangs with every step. After completing the simple task, I returned to my bedroom. As I was grabbing the crutches, the doorbell rang.

Out of breath from the arduous trip down the stairs, I stopped to look in the peephole before I swung open the front door saying, "Sorry for the delay. It took me a while to maneuver the steps."

"I tried coming in through the garage, but the bay door was locked."

"It's automatic for me to keep the place secure."

"I'm surprised you don't have an alarm system."

I shrugged my shoulders not wanting him to know about my aversion. When I returned from Japan, I felt like a prisoner in my home. My stepdad had installed a security system claiming it would keep criminals out. As soon as we were inside the house, he locked all the doors and windows. In doing so, neighbors couldn't hear his intimidating tone as he shouted out a list of rules he insisted I had to follow. He warned if I tried to leave without his permission, in an instant a beeping would alert him to where the breach had occurred. Armed with the exact location, he'd quickly stop me and serious consequences would follow.

I gazed at Jack's arms laden with shopping bags. "Looks like you have enough groceries for a week."

"Maybe for you, but with a teen aboard my guess is this stuff won't last long."

He placed the bags on the counter and removed a large handle bag from the local burger place from his wrist.

I started to unload items, but he stopped me. "Let me," he said, "you need to rest your leg."

I moved to the side and allowed him to unpack.

"This is fantastic. Guess you surmised with me living alone, eating out a lot, and skipping meals due to long work hours I wouldn't keep the house stocked." I asked, "Do you live alone?"

"Yup, I do, but I like to cook. I find baking especially relaxing, but by the looks of you my guess is you're not fond of sweets."

"Was when I was Charley's age or I thought I did. Maybe I just ate junk food..."

"As comfort food?"

His accurate insight made me uneasy. I hoped his powers of perception extended to him realizing I'd prefer to keep parts of my past private.

Dismissively I said, "I'm sure you have a ton of work to do. You don't have to stay."

"Are you asking me to leave, before we eat?"

"I'm sorry. I just meant I didn't want to put you out any more than I already have. By the way, how much do I owe you for the gas you used for the round trip to Yosemite and for all this food?"

"Nothing," he said while shaking his head. "It was a pleasant drive and I had fun loading the grocery basket with things I've denied myself for years. And I can assure you, spending time with you is no bother. Haven't you noticed I've been interested in getting to know you for some time?"

He sounded sincere, but a niggling in the back of my head made me doubt him. I turned away and began setting the table.

He pulled out a chair. With a wave of his arm, he indicated I sit down. He took the stack of dishes out of my hands and placed them, flatware, and the bag with our lunch on the table.

His words surprised me.

"I sensed you were exceptional and now I'm sure of it."

Thinking his compliment was some cheap line, I didn't respond.

"Not everyone would open their home to a teenager, especially a troubled one."

I barked at him. "She's only here temporarily until she decides where she'd like to be. Besides, she's not responsible for her dire situation or her emotional turmoil. Anyone would be a wreck if they experienced similar traumas."

As if to embrace me, with outstretched arms he knelt down next to me. He stopped two feet from me and lowered his hands. "I wasn't being critical of her. I apologize if I came off sounding insensitive. Remember me? I'm the guy who'd like to help Charley bring her abuser to justice."

"I'm the one who needs to apologize. I'm just a little on edge. I'm afraid I don't know how to care for Charley. Parenting is foreign to me."

"Most people are amateurs in the childrearing department. Guess most folks learn as they go."

A veil of sadness fell over my heart. "But at whose expense?"

"Why doubt yourself? You're doing great so far."

"How would you know?"

"In my years as a defense attorney, I've seen my share of unhealthy families. It's made me realize how lucky

I am to have good parents, people who have been and still are open to learning. I'm one of the lucky ones who felt loved. Don't get me wrong they're not perfect. They have their idiosyncrasies just like anyone else and I wasn't the ideal kid. I gave them a ration of worries."

"Really?"

He nodded, "First, I was bored in school. At Charley's age, I cut classes and didn't do my assignments. My parents kept encouraging me just to get through high school. Being successful professionals, they made it clear they had big plans for my future. Maybe, that's why I rebelled. Unfortunately they didn't have much influence over me."

"What made you turn around?"

"Nothing noble or enlightening."

"Then what?"

"I had a crush on the most popular girl in school. Her father was a successful businessman her mother a real stunner. They lived in the biggest house in town. She was pretty and smart. The guy she was dating was two years older than us someone slated to be most likely to succeed. After he graduated, I decided I'd take his place in her life. In order to get her attention, I had to clean up my act, get good grades, and somehow become college material. The more I focused on her the less time I spent with my friends getting into trouble.

"I started going to a church youth group because she was a member. I joined the debate team to show her how bright I was. I tried out for sports and miraculously made the wrestling team. I was involved in so many things on campus I didn't even think of cutting classes. Rather than sneaking alcohol or puffing cigarettes, I got high on cramming for tests, polishing essays, and playing in tournaments.

"Ironically, in the process of finding my calling, I lost interest in her. In the end, I didn't find her preoccupation with herself very attractive."

"I see you haven't changed. When you want something, you go after it."

"True but now I don't go after fluff. I'd like to think I matured enough to see beyond the superficial. Now I go after the real article the complete package: physical beauty, smarts, and an irresistible soul like yours." He reached up and brushed his lips on my cheek.

In the next moment, he stood and left the room.

As if to seal in the glorious warmth, my right hand covered the spot where he'd almost kissed me.

# Chapter Twenty-Six
## Charley

Jack knocked on the closed door. "I need your help."

I wondered what he meant.

"Sam thinks I bought too much food. Come upstairs and prove her wrong."

Fearing being alone in a bedroom with a man, before he had a chance to enter I jumped up flung open the door and rushed past him.

On my way up the stairs, one whiff of greasy fries triggered an appetite I thought was gone forever. At the same time, I didn't want to eat. Hoping the horrible pain of loss would end I stopped moving, lowered my head, and wished I could melt into the walls never to exist again.

Without looking up from the grained hardwood floor, I heard Jack dash past me. He said, "We'll be in the kitchen waiting for you."

Despite my deep sadness, I couldn't ignore my rumbling stomach.

Finally, I followed my nose, but lingered at the second story landing and listened to Sam saying, "I should go to her. Bring her some food. Maybe she'd prefer eating alone."

"Relax. Charley will be here soon."

I peeked from the kitchen into the breakfast nook and saw Sam nervously tapping her fingers on the table.

Jack grabbed a pillow from the living room couch, placed it on the seat of the chair opposite Sam. From under the table, he lifted her wrapped ankle and gently lowered it onto the softness.

"I'll check on Charley," he said.

I walked into the room saying, "I'm right here."

Jack waved his hand toward the table. "Take a seat. We have some serious eating to do."

We sat around stuffing our faces with drippy burgers and dipping fries into ranch dressing.

When I slugged the last drop of my shake, Jack quickly jumped up and took another out of the refrigerator. "I got an extra just in case. Hope vanilla will do."

He asked us, "Well what do two you think of my favorite burger joint?"

Bobbing her head up and down, Sam pointed to her mouth indicating it was too full to speak.

He turned to me.

Although I thought they were great burgers, I just smiled figuring it was safer to be quiet rather than risking annoying one or both of them.

Jack rose. "Don't either of you move."

Sam and I didn't argue with him. As he cleared the table. I thought I was watching a sitcom where, as Mike would say, the man did woman's work.

While Jack washed the few dishes, he seemed happy whistling a tune I couldn't identify. What a difference from what happened at my house.

I thought of Mike, the lazy bozo ordering us around. Of us waiting on him like we were his slaves. He never cared if Mom was tired or sick. He didn't do squat other than demand we give him whatever he wanted. Despite us doing all the chores, he was always in a bad mood. He was always a grouch.

Jack suggested, "Let's play cards."

Sam said, "I don't have a deck."

"No worries. While I was out, I picked up a little something I'm sure we'll all enjoy."

After pulling the strings of a plastic trash bag, he lifted it saying, "I'll dump this in the garbage can I saw in the garage and be right back.

This was my chance to escape. "Thank you, Sam, for letting me stay here. Please thank Jack for the burger and fries."

She answered, "You're welcome. Is there anything else I can get for you?"

I wanted to bolt, but Jack returned and handed me a box. It was a monopoly game. I frowned at him. Did he think I was a kid?

"You can be banker," he said.

Since I didn't have anything better to do, I ripped off the cellophane and opened the box. Not having played in years I had to check the instructions before giving out the fake money.

He put a bowl filled with chips and three cokes on the table.

I waited for Jack and Sam to choose their tokens. We each picked one of the new additions. She took the penguin, he took the rubber duck, and I took the tyrannosaurus.

A part of me wanted to watch Jack, waiting for him to fall into the usual man routine. I figured he'd only been helpful to gain points with Sam, but sooner rather than later, he'd show his selfish side.

Sam brought up her favorite music group. Jack jumped right in with a list of popular songs he enjoyed.

They seemed to be up on what was happening now rather bragging about the oldies.

The conversation shifted to movies. Usually trapped in the house, I spent hours glued to the TV set.

"What's your favorite show," Jack asked.

I couldn't believe I told them, "Hallmark Movie Channel." I must've sounded like a nerd.

Sam said, "Guess we're hopeless romantics. It's my favorite, too."

I found myself laughing.

*Was I really having fun?*

*How could I be playing a silly game when my baby was dead?*

Guilt like a heavy wet blanket fell over me.

My change in mood must've been obvious.

"You okay?" Sam asked.

Jack tried to get my mind back on the game. I heard him say, "Charley, looks like you have a chance to wipe me out."

I thought, *Who were these strangers and what did they want from me?*

*What was in it for them?*

*Was I their latest pet project?*

All I had to do to join my daughter was to run up the next flight of stairs and jump out a window.

*Who am I kidding?* No matter when or how I died, I wouldn't be going to the special place God saved for her. No. God wouldn't make room for me in Heaven. He'd send me straight to hell where I belonged.

Maybe I was already there. Nothing seemed real here. I felt feverish. I began to shiver feeling cold, empty, and dizzy.

Jack's strong arms helped me lie down on the couch.

"I'll get you some water," I heard Sam say.

Closing my eyes, I tried to tune them out.

I saw my sleeping baby wrapped in a pink blanket floating in the clear blue sky. I told her, "Oh my dear little girl, I'm sorry I failed you. I'm sorry I caused your death. I'm sorry I only thought about me getting away from Mike. Sorry I didn't think of the terrible life you'd have with me living on the streets not having money to support you.

"You're lucky not to have a worthless mother like me. Maybe God will send you to a deserving mother. A grown-up woman who's married to a nice guy who loves her. Maybe your new mother will be able to gloat about expecting you. Maybe your father will paint your room and buy a nice crib for you to sleep in. Maybe your grandmother will crochet booties for you. Maybe you'll have a real chance at happiness."

I turned away from my child and looked upward, "Oh God, please don't punish my little one for my sins. Give her a good life filled with love.

"She didn't deserve having a pervert for a father or a loser for a mother. I hope in Your wisdom you figured it out. You realized she deserves better than what she had or maybe you gave her a choice of staying with me or leaving. Maybe she wisely chose to flee my dirty body. Maybe You let her decide. Maybe You gave her a preview of the horrible life she would've had with me. Maybe You spared her.

"Oh please dear God, don't let her really lose her chance at life. Please dear God, do what you want with me, but give my innocent babe happiness."

# Chapter Twenty-Seven
## Sam

I rushed to the sink and filled a glass with water. My haste accentuated my limping and caused more water to spill out of the glass than what remained in it.

By the time I reached the couch, Charley had dozed off.

I studied her sleeping form.

A rare sweetness like a halo radiated perfection around her face.

My heart as if having wings fluttered in my chest. I felt privileged to be her caretaker albeit a temporary one.

I marveled at her unique beauty.

Overcome with a glowing sensation deep within me I wondered if this was how a healthy parent felt each day about her child's existence.

I thought of Charley's mother. She had to be an emotionally injured soul to overlook the miracle of her daughter. Nevertheless, I wondered how she could choose not to protect her precious child.

Charley was strong and confident when I found her. She was determined and capable. She didn't shrivel up into a ball and roll into a corner. She didn't ignore her problems. She faced her pregnancy and made the courageous decision to keep her baby. In her desperate desire to save her child from Mike or a foster home, Charley devised an escape plan.

Despite her mother's lack of support, with Charley's strength I felt hopeful she'd recover. I felt certain, away from Mike, she could have a productive happy future.

I couldn't help but compare Charley to me. We both had horrific memories of violation and we both ran away.

I peered at Charley and realized how young I was when my stepdad selfishly stole my innocence.

An avalanche of fear came crashing down on my heart reopening scars from old wounds.

Like me, because of what one perverted man had done, would Charley continue to avoid close relationships with all men?

Uncontrollable tears gushed from my eyes splashing my face with a sorrow I'd kept bottled up for years.

Entirely forgetting Jack's presence, I jumped when he attempted to put his arms around me.

Respecting my reaction, he stepped back.

Without speaking, I felt him offering me comfort.

Realizing he wasn't going to hurt me, I allowed myself to slip into his embrace.

His touch reminded me of a time long ago when I felt safe in my father's arms.

Surprising myself, between sobs, I told Jack, "I can relate to Charley. We both had stepfathers who did evil things to us. While my mother defended her new husband, my father saved me by sending me to a boarding school away from my wicked stepdad and my non-protective mother."

I gulped down the pain of maternal abandonment. "My stepdad only hurt me for a little while, but I'm the one who tossed the subsequent years away. I hid from the world. Not trusting too many people, I buried myself in books and legal documents."

Without saying a word, Jack conveyed his sympathy by gently stroking my hair.

"I don't want Charley to be like me." I moved back and took his hands in mine. "I don't want her to turn away sincere honest good men. I don't want her to deny herself the experiences of falling in love, marrying, and having children."

I stared at his strong reassuring face. His eyes beckoned me into a tranquil sea leading to a peaceful paradise.

*Was it possible for him to provide security or was I deluding myself?*

I told him, "Since I met Charley, I feel as if I'm noticing people for the first time."

He leaned closer and brushed his cheek with mine.

I whispered, "Let's go out on the back patio while Charley sleeps."

To take the weight off my injured leg I leaned on Jack's arm. I led the way out the sliding door to a small table flanked with two metal chairs atop the green, lush lawn.

He waited until I was safely sitting before he pulled a chair closer and sat facing me.

I asked him, "How can I ever repay you for your kind friendship?"

He smiled. "When your ankle heals how about allowing me to date you?"

I sighed. "I don't think it's a good idea for us to see each other socially."

"Why not?"

"Because we work in the same building."

"Not for long. I've given my resignation and will be opening a solo practice in a month."

"Why? I thought with your superb reputation for winning cases you'd make partner soon. Isn't that why you're with the firm?"

"No. That's never been my intention. Like any rookie attorney, I needed to put theories into practice. After ten years, I feel I've gained enough experience to make it on my own. Despite the pressures and the low moments, being a defense attorney is an ideal match for my personality. I can't wait to choose my clients, my cases."

"That's really exciting."

"What about you? What are your career plans?"

I shrugged my shoulders. "Guess I'm content for now. I really haven't given the future much thought."

"Really?"

"Well." I realized I hadn't shared my musings with anyone. "I've always wondered what it would be like to be an investigative attorney. I'm interested in criminal law, but know I wouldn't feel comfortable in a courtroom addressing a judge and jury. Since I want to get involved in cases but want to stay in the background doing independent investigations might be a rewarding place to start."

I reached down and raked the grass. I plucked a blade from its root and twirled it in my hand. It felt soft and delicate. I smelled its freshness.

I grabbed another and instantly compared the two. One ended in a point. The other had a slanted end. I gazed up at the Fremont cottonwood dominating the courtyard. Its heart shaped leaves were dancing in the breeze. Was each white veined leaf different? If so, how had I missed seeing variations? Had I been living in a fog limiting my view of natural phenomenon including the beauty growing in my own backyard?

Although I'd heard it many times before, today was the day I realized no two things were alike.

Had I dumped all men together in an unsavory categorical pot?

What a fool I'd been not to marvel at their differences.

I gazed into Jack's green eyes. They sparkled with energy.

He wasn't just another lawyer or another man. He was a one of a kind individual. Just as there wasn't and never would be another Charley or another me there would never be another Jack.

I was in awe of the realization of reality. It was far more vivid than a painting. It was far more lyrical than a poem. It was far more moving than a sentimental tune.

God's creations were far greater than anything anyone could imagine.

For too long, I'd refused to look at the specialness around me. An example was not paying attention to the magnificent forest.

Jack offered, "Anytime you want to get your feet wet there'll be a place for you in my office."

"I'll keep your offer in mind and yes I'd love to go out on a date with you."

I immediately questioned my decision.

Maybe my conflicted feelings showed on my face, because Jack said, "Before you change your mind, I'm going to leave you to rest."

When he stood, an image of a pine tree flashed in my mind. Suddenly, I thought like the pine Jack was tall, complex, flexible, and his crown had its own magnificent presence.

# Chapter Twenty-Eight
## Charley

It felt like one of the sleepovers I'd seen in movies, but never had. Sam and I sat in pajamas topping off our pizza dinner with a bowl of popcorn nestled between us while we watched a horror film.

She'd been good about not asking questions or lecturing. As the days passed, I almost felt comfortable in her modern home. I almost stopped thinking of my lost baby. I almost stopped fearing Mike.

Before we turned in for the night, I told Sam, "Your place looks like a House and Garden TV show. Everything is so perfect, so new. Aren't you worried I'll make a mess or ruin your stuff?"

"They're only things meant to be used and enjoyed." She winked. "I'm glad you're here. It feels good to share my home with someone as dear as you."

"Thank you. I won't stay long and I'll be extra careful. I promise. Just tell me what you want me to do to earn my keep."

"You're my guest. You're welcome to stay here until... Any ideas of where you'd like to go?"

"I'm planning to get a job and become an emancipated minor."

"What about high school? Don't you want to graduate and go to college?"

"I need to take care of myself like you do."

"Having earned a law degree and establishing a career is how I'm able to pay for the things I need and want."

"But I can't go back to school. Everyone probably knows about what happened?"

"Who would've told them?"

"Mike said, many times, if I ever tried to get away he'd spread ugly rumors about me. He'd ruin my reputation."

"If you believe he'll do that, what do you have to lose by pressing charges against him?"

"My life. Mike will kill me if I tell the police what he did."

"I thought you said no one would believe you because Mike is the pillar of society."

"It's true. No one would even question him. People think he's some kind of a holy man." I started to tremble. I raised my voice. "You don't know him. You don't know how good he is at fooling folks."

"You can go to a different school."

"Like I said, you don't know him. He'll find me wherever I am."

As if a light went on in my head, I saw things clearly and I felt my insides shaking. "Sam he'll soon come after me. Having me here isn't safe for you. I should go right away."

"Surely, he'd be worried about getting caught if he tried anything that foolish."

"You don't get it. He thinks he can get away with anything and he has so far. He thinks he's special. And maybe he is because people in our church almost worship him."

"How about taking classes in an alternative setting, like home schooling?"

I didn't know how to get through to her. "You're not listening to me. Mike will never let me get away with leaving him. Someday soon, he'll come after me and punish me. He'll torture me. If I should die in the process, it won't matter, because nothing can hurt his precious image. Mike is the kind of guy who could get away with murder."

I stood up ready to run away. "That's why I can't stay here. I can't let him hurt you. I've already lost my baby. I don't want to lose the only friend I've ever had."

When she stood and inched closer to me, I saw tears running down her cheeks, but her voice sounded steady. "I didn't have a loving mother and I don't know the first thing about being a parent. Yet, I'm sure I can provide for you. I'm offering you a home not just to help you in the moment but forever."

"Don't say things you don't mean, can't mean. I don't blame you, but sooner than you can imagine you'll get tired of having me around."

"That's not true. I'm in your debt for helping me wake up. Since my stepdad molested me, I tried to escape him by sleepwalking through life. My fear of pain was so great I didn't allow myself to feel pleasure."

She reached out her arms and rested her hands on my clasped pair. "Since I met you, Charley, I realized it wasn't my stepfather's fault I isolated myself. It wasn't my mother's lack of protection that made me fearful. I was the one who turned away from fun and exploration. I chose to squirrel away in an office where I hoped no one would notice me, where I didn't do anything of great value. As a result, I wasn't a nice person. I was selfish and worst of all I was afraid of people. I feared they'd hurt my feelings, tear out my heart, and violate my body. I'd spent my life hiding from all of God's creations. I isolated myself, drowned myself in my studies and now in my work, work I don't enjoy but treasure because it's my hideaway from humanity. From now on, I refuse to assume the role of a victim. I refuse to be a defeated, wounded, lame little creature, terrified of life and petrified of death."

*What was that about? What the heck was she ranting about?* "While I can't take credit for your revelation, I'm happy for you, but our situations are different. Your stepfather was a bad man, but not a maniac like Mike. Your stepfather may have gone on to hurt other people, but he left you alone. Mike won't move on without destroying me."

"Let's pray for God to intervene." She lowered her head in silent prayer.

I too asked for the Lord's help.

Maybe Sam couldn't understand my feelings. Maybe she couldn't realize just how dangerous Mike really was. Although I knew she couldn't save me, and couldn't change what was to come, her offering me hope felt good, really good.

# Chapter Twenty-Nine
## Sam

My supervisor had authorized my request of taking a week of sick leave in order to give my ankle time to heal. He and I worked out a plan where after I returned to work I'd do much of my assignments remotely from home. Trudy was eager to do whatever she could to help. Savvy about computer technology she set up an encrypted email program. This would protect client confidentiality when she sent me their files.

I suggested Charley see a psychologist to deal with her traumas. She wisely pointed out, "Now that you remember more bad stuff about your past why don't you see a therapist, too."

From then on, we attended weekly sessions with separate psychologists. In addition, I was extremely busy taking Charley clothes shopping, food shopping, and shopping for items to personalize her room. All the while, I wondered how parents of large families managed to have the time and money to care for several children.

It felt as if Charley was the sister I never had and I hoped I acted more like her contemporary than a parent figure. We laughed a lot. Sat on each other's beds painting each other's nails. Watched movies, listened to our favorite music albums, and took yoga classes together.

Without solicitation, Charley gave me her candid opinion. "You ought to wear more flattering clothes. Why are you hiding your great figure in loose fitting outfits?"

With her help, I changed my style from matronly to fashionably modern. The professional suits I purchased emphasized my tiny waist and showed off my long legs.

Most of all, in my free time, I loved wearing feminine apparel: flimsy tops, lacy skirts, spaghetti strapped dresses. I even changed my footwear to include high heel and flat sandals so I could show off the toe rings Charley insisted I buy.

When she raved about my new look, I jokingly told her, "It feels marvelous flaunting my God given assets."

From out of nowhere, Charley asked me, "Are you afraid living alone?"

"No."

"But what if someone breaks in?"

"The odds are against that happening, but just in case I keep two guns in the house."

"Really?"

"Years ago, I went through a fearful period, couldn't sleep, and jumped at every little sound. My therapist at the time had recommended I go to a range and hire an instructor to teach me how to shoot."

"How did it feel to hit a bull's eye?"

I didn't want to describe the fantasies I had of blasting any fool who tried to lay a hand on me.

I shared, "While becoming proficient in using a firearm I gained self-confidence and felt empowered. Somehow shooting up targets helped me let go of my rage."

"Will you take me for lessons?"

"I'll take you to a shooting range when your therapist thinks you're ready to unleash your anger safely."

At home, after her lessons and assignments were completed, we experimented baking and preparing meals.

Day by day, it felt as if I was watching time lapsed photography of an unfurling flower. As Charley opened up emotionally, she blossomed into a stunning young woman. Her warm smile reflected her inner nature. She was helpful, cheerful, and extremely intelligent.

Jack called daily asking if he could stop by. Not wanting Charley to think he was a permanent fixture, despite how much I enjoyed his company, I limited his visits to two nights a week and either a Saturday or Sunday on weekends when we pooled our ideas and took day trips. He always insisted on driving, taking us to San Francisco, Sacramento, and towns in between.

More than once Charley told us it was a treat to see other places, because in the past she'd seldom left Stockton.

During our excursions, a pattern emerged. Charley glommed onto protective objects. In San Francisco's Chinatown, she paused to stare at a row of imperial guardian lions. "These look impressive," she said.

Jack pointed to a sign stating from 206 BC people believed these lions, usually depicted in pairs with a male and a female, had powerful protective benefits.

He added, "Westerners often mislabeled the lions as foo dogs."

"I wish I had one to protect me from..." Her voice trailed off, but I knew she was still terrified of Mike.

Jack said, "I think that's a splendid idea. Pick the one you like."

"Really," she squealed.

He nodded.

She fingered a keychain with a dangling lion.

"How about something a bit bigger to keep evil from harming you at home?"

Her eyes stared at the largest statue, but after a few seconds, she walked to the other end of the shelf and pointed to a diminutive one.

Jack hadn't missed her subtle attention to the huge statue. He picked it up. "Now we're talking protection." He asked a salesperson to help locate its mate.

"This one is male lion. See he's holding ball under left paw. Put him on left side as you're looking out of door." The salesperson pushed a few statues aside until he picked up another one. "This is female lion. See she's holding cub under right paw. Put her on opposite side of male."

I said, "They look heavy."

The man said, "Good thing you have strong man with you."

After paying for them, Jack insisted on carrying the wrapped stone statues through the crowded streets to the garage where he'd parked his car.

While he was putting them in his trunk, Charley asked, "If it's okay with you, Sam, I'd like to put them outside my bedroom door so they can guard you and me."

"Of course. A little extra protection couldn't hurt." I hoped it was prudent to indulge her inordinate fear of Mike breaking in and harming her.

When we spent the day at Indian Grinding Rock State Park, she searched for the perfect woven dreamcatcher to put over her headboard.

At Victorian mansions we toured she hurried into gift shops asking if there were gargoyle statues for sale.

She liked wearing onyx jewelry to defend against the evil eye and avert danger. She also wore pearls to protect against fire. She collected key chains each with a protective charm.

Although Jack and I bought her these items, I feared we were feeding her paranoid obsession of Mike one day coming after her.

Jack compared her obsession with a baby clinging to a certain blanket or needing a nightlight to fall asleep. "What harm could it do? Helping her feel safe is all that matters. My guess is with time she'll outgrow fearing Mike."

In Lake Tahoe, I was pleased when all she wanted was a snow globe of a cabin in the woods. She told me, "I once had a snow globe, but Mike smashed it."

I assured her, "Guaranteed he'll never get his hands on this one."

On our first visit to Jack's place, I was pleasantly surprised. We pulled up to a vintage Craftsman style house built in 1916. We stepped inside and Charley asked for a grand tour. Grand indeed described its appearance. He'd restored the interior to its glory days and furnished the rooms with lovely antiques.

We both complimented his excellent taste.

Charley asked, "Did someone help you decorate?"

"In a way. As a kid, I had fun tagging along with my mom to garage sales. We played a game pretending to hear stories of the past from interesting pieces we found."

"I get it," Charley said. "Ever hear a horror story?"

"Anything I didn't like gave me the willies."

At dinner, Charley couldn't stop praising him for making the best macaroni and cheese she'd ever had.

He responded, "Funny I couldn't help noticing the face you made when I took the pan out of the oven."

"Well I'd never seen my favorite dish looking so pale. I thought you were trying to pawn off some bland white sauce pasta."

"Well now you know Wisconsin white cheddar is sharp and flavorful. Wait until you try a wedge with a hot slice of my Dutch apple crumb pie."

After two heaping helpings of macaroni, I thought she'd be too full to have dessert, but he was right about her being over the moon when she took a bite of the cheese with a forkful of pie.

I asked Charley if she felt comfortable with Jack hanging out with us.

She teased, "Sure. I like having him be our official guinea pig sampling what we prepare." Or she'd say, "Having him around gives me a chance to pick on someone other than you."

One morning at breakfast, I casually asked her what she thought of Jack. "I value your opinion so be completely honest."

Without hesitation she rambled, "He's fun. He doesn't raise his voice. He doesn't cuss. He jumps right in ready to help. He doesn't brag. He's not like perverted Mike trying to con people into believing he's holier than thou.

"Jack's a hunk. He's successful. He owns a real nice place and a great car. From the way, he keeps his house and the way he cooks, it's clear he doesn't need a woman to take care of him. And he really seems to like you. Do you feel the same way about him?"

If I were honest, I'd describe my feelings akin to my memories of riding ocean waves with my dad. My emotions vacillated between exhilaration and terror. I felt safe in his presence, but feared slipping out of his grasp. I envisioned the undulating mountain of water crashing down on me and carrying me out to bottomless depths. When I was with Jack, I delighted in having wild passionate fantasies of him one minute and dreaded my feelings of extreme vulnerability the next. Although I had trepidations of him abandoning me like my father had done and drowning me in unfathomable pain, I didn't want to miss the excitement of being with Jack.

I told Charley, "Sure. So far, he seems like a wonderful man, but time will tell. Won't it? Time and circumstance always bring out the real person. What does your gut tell you about Jack?"

"From the start, he seemed nice. At first, I wondered if he was playacting. Guys usually treated my mom okay until they got her under the sheets. Mike was the same. When they hooked up, he started taking advantage of her and ordering her around. Of course I don't know how intimate you two are."

When she looked at me I tried not to laugh, but couldn't help myself. "Not that it's any of your business but we haven't even kissed."

Her eyes widened, but she couldn't suppress her giggles. "Why not?"

"I want to take things slow."

She nodded as if knowing exactly why not rushing a physical romance was important to me.

Charley said, "Mike wouldn't wait for a time when a woman was ready. One way or another he'd get what he wanted when he wanted it. And another big difference between Jack and Mike is Mike only pretended to like me in front of my mom. Once her back was turned, he was a total creep. Come to think of it, he never, not even once treated me as good as Jack does."

Her next words echoed my thoughts. "Jack seems respectful. I don't know. I'm confused. Are there any good men? I know you like him so I hope for your sake Jack's a decent guy. Guess I think he really likes you because of the many tiny things he does for you and for me."

"I'll admit I'm attracted to him. He's kind, handsome, and seductive, but like you, I'm automatically leery of him because he's a man. As much as I don't want the past to cloud my perception, I'm not sure I can trust my heart."

"Why don't you go out with him just you two?"

I shrugged my shoulders.

"Hope it's not because you don't want to leave me alone."

I must have hesitated too long, because she said, "Would you go out with him while I went to a church youth group meeting?"

"I appreciate your offer and I'm sure you'd have fun, but I respect your concern about Mike having tainted your reputation."

"You're the one who assured me, no one, not even Trudy knows about my pregnancy and miscarriage."

"Yes. That's true."

"And you've told me Trudy hasn't heard any negative tales about me from the other kids."

"Correct."

"And you're the one who has sacrificed going to services because of my refusal to set foot in a place that respects Mike."

"I'm not making any sacrifices for you. From the moment I saw you, I knew you were extraordinary. Every day since you've proven me right. I've willingly chosen not to expose you to Mike in order to protect you, because I love you."

She fell into my arms and hugged me tight. "I love you, too."

Tears of joy sprang from my eyes.

She let go and said, "I want to go to tomorrow night's meeting and I'd like you to call Jack and ask him out on a date. You keep telling me to stop living in fear. Now I'm telling you to show me how by dating Jack."

"You got me," I said.

The next night, as we pulled into the church's parking lot assuming I was feeling like a mother leaving her little one at school for the first time, I tried to ignore my stomach churning with anxiety.

When I walked Charley to the door, the teens warmly welcomed her.

She winked at me and broadened her smile. "Don't you believe I can be okay for a few hours on my own?"

Her rhetorical question made it easy for me to return to Jack who was waiting in his car.

# Chapter Thirty
## Charley

Not wanting Mom to know where Sam lived, I met her outside her work, a big box store warehouse. She'd been there for years yanking down packages off shelves filling orders. Mike was happy about the overtime hours usually available. Being extremely jealous, he approved of her having mostly female coworkers.

When she came out the door, she ran to me and gave me a big bear hug. "You're looking good."

With dark bags under her eyes, I couldn't honestly return the compliment. "Mom I'm worried you're working too hard. When are you going on vacation?"

"I'm fine and looking forward to traveling with Mike soon."

"Where're you going?"

"It's a surprise. Mike's making all the arrangements, but he told me I'll need a swimsuit."

Long sleeves concealed her arms and she was wearing jeans. My guess was she was covering up recent bruises. I wanted to tell her I knew he'd been hitting her, but was sure she'd deny it or defend him in some way. I thought of the times she took the blame for his slaps and punches. Like a parrot, she repeated a familiar refrain. "It was my fault Mike was upset. It was my fault Mike hit me."

By now, I knew it was useless to try to change the way she saw things where Mike was concerned.

She squeezed a wad of bills in my hand. "I managed to hide away a few dollars. Maybe you can give it to the church lady so she can keep you longer. Things are going real good with Mike and I right now and I wouldn't want you coming home to spoil our romance."

"It's okay, Mom. I don't want to come back not with Mike there."

"He said you could come to dinner and pick up your things if you want. He said you could move back after a while."

I swallowed back my anger. Sure, he'd like me to come by so he could threaten me. Sure, he'd like me to go to my room where he could hurt me again.

She kept talking, "He said he'd like to see you in church and hopes you'll beg for God's forgiveness."

I didn't think I could stand there a second longer listening to another glowing word about disgusting Mike. Why couldn't Mom be like Sam? Without me saying much, Sam understood why I hated Mike. Why couldn't Mom believe me and despise him because of what he'd done to me?

Fortunately, she said, "I gotta go. You know how Mike is. He'll want to know why I'm late. Besides I have to get dinner started or there'll be trouble."

I kissed her cheek wishing I could take her away from her mean no good husband. I felt so sorry for her making such a horrible mistake being with him. "Mom, be careful."

"Sure, you too baby girl."

Looking at her dashing away, I realized only she could help herself and wondered why she didn't.

Seeing Mom reminded me of a time not too long ago, when I felt dirty because of the garbage Mike spewed out at me. If it hadn't been for Sam treating me like I was okay I'd still think I was trash and by now be in the gutter.

It wasn't until I was back in the comforts of Sam's house that I thought about Mom not giving a hoot about her one and only daughter.

I wished I could do something to make her love me. If only I was smarter, prettier.

Maybe I could get a job and together we could afford to rent an apartment. Maybe then, she wouldn't feel she needed Mike. My therapist explained if Mom didn't think she needed Mike, he wouldn't be able to use her.

Oh, how I missed Mom.

How I wished she'd want to be with me.

Didn't she know I needed her?

Suddenly I understood the homework assignment my therapist had given me. She'd told me I could want people in my life, but the truth was I didn't need anyone to make me happy. She told me to repeat a hundred times a day, "All I need is me."

# Chapter Thirty-One
## Sam

Feasting on life's sweetness as if it were a cinnamon bun, I didn't think about its sticky side.

Once Charley successfully returned to school, I established a routine of driving her there before going to my office. I picked her up after classes and worked remotely from home for a few hours while she did her homework.

Jack set up his own law practice. Since he didn't have a heavy caseload, he often met me for lunch and stopped by a few nights a week. The three of us spent weekends together at my place, his place, or out exploring.

Charley teased us. "Jack and Sam are sweethearts."

When I checked with her to see if she was okay having Jack around her reply was, "I feel we three are connected." She'd add, "Connected in good ways."

She told me, "Don't think I'm a bad person. It's not that I don't love my mom, but I wish you had permanent custody of me. I know that even if my mom left Mike she'd find another bad guy to be with." She started crying. "I don't want to have to live with her ever again."

Jack prepared the necessary papers and presented them to Charley's mother. To my surprise, her mother signed over custody. Maybe it was my suspicious nature, but I wondered if she asked Jack for a cash incentive. And I wouldn't have been surprised if he fulfilled her request.

Charley seemed pleased with her mother's decision. Although it was what she had asked for, I suspected her mother's abandonment had to be extremely painful. But Charley didn't say so.

Enjoying each day, I'd grown complacent. Charley on the other hand was vigilant. Once she learned Jack was handy, she asked him to install a deadbolt on her bedroom door. All these months later, she continued to lock it before going to sleep.

One morning I found her in the kitchen holding the gun I'd stowed away in the back of a stack of seldom-used dishes.

She said as she placed it in my hands, "I can see from your frightened expression that it's loaded, but why did you hide it?"

"I didn't want to risk you getting hurt."

She shouted, "Don't you want me to have a way to protect myself? What if Mike shows up? He's always armed with anger and his strong hands are powerful weapons."

Her breathing was ragged. "You haven't kept your promise. You haven't taken me to a shooting range. Until you do, I want you to leave the gun where I can easily reach it. If that pervert shows up I don't think I'll have a problem pointing it and pulling the trigger until he'd dead."

In order to calm her, I temporarily put the gun in the nearest drawer.

She asked, "Is your other gun still on the top shelf of your closet?"

Annoyed about her having searched through my things I didn't dare speak for fear I'd criticize her. Instead, I nodded. I didn't tell her that gun wasn't loaded, but I guessed she'd also found boxes of clips storing rounds of ammunition.

A few days later just as I parked in front of her high school, she announced, "I'm going on a date Saturday night."

Nervously I asked, "With whom?"

"A cool guy."

I wanted to tell her she was too young to date, but didn't want to alienate her.

"Is he a student here?"

"No."

"Is he in your youth group?"

"No. I met him through my friend, Jean."

"How old is he?"

"Nineteen."

"Is he in college?"

"No. He works and has a car."

"Where are you going?"

"To a party."

Images of alcohol and drugs from marijuana to cocaine paraded in my mind. The thought of them drinking and this man driving terrified me. I blurted, "I can't allow you to go."

She opened the car door, jumped out, and yelled, "You're not my mother so you can't stop me. And don't bother to pick me up today. I can get my own ride home." She slammed the door shut.

I sat there taking deep breaths, but couldn't hold back my tears.

The sound of a beeping horn reminded me I was blocking the way. I eased away from the curb and drove a few blocks before parking. I reached for my cell, called Jack, and told him what had happened.

"Don't worry. Tonight you can explain your concerns calmly."

"You didn't hear her hateful tone. After all I've done for her, how could she speak to me like that?"

"Do you take care of her to win her favor? Did you take her into your home let her into your heart in order to gain her appreciation?"

"No. Of course not."

"Why are you so upset about how she spoke to you? Sounds like you were interrogating her. Sounds like you were accusing her of bad behavior."

"Me? I'm just worried she's too vulnerable to be with a man, an older one at that."

"So you don't trust her?"

"She's emotionally fragile."

"And what about you? Mature parents have to have thick skin."

"Are you saying I acted like a child?"

"No. I'm trying to determine why you're upset."

"Because I'm hurt. I love her as if she were my daughter but realize she doesn't see me as a mother figure."

"Well I disagree. I think she's just a normal teenager rebelling against a very controlling mom."

I laughed. "How can I play this game when there aren't any ground rules?"

# Chapter Thirty-Two
## Charley

Why was Sam mean to me? I thought she understood me, trusted me, even loved me, but just now she treated me like I'm a little kid, someone else's kid.

Was I clueless? Was I just her do-good deed of the year? Would she dump me the first time I disagreed with her or when a more interesting charity case came along? Would she send me packing back to Mom or to a fancy boarding school?

I wanted her to find happiness. I wanted her to fall in love. Like the men in all the romance stories, I wanted Jack to be a decent guy.

He seemed like the real deal, but maybe he had other motives. Maybe he acted nice because he wanted something. Maybe unlike Mike, Jack was patient waiting for his prize.

How could I trust strangers, when my own mom didn't care about me or want me? It didn't make sense for Sam and Jack to give a darn about me.

They weren't family. They didn't have any ties to me. They didn't have any obligation to look after me or keep me in their lives. Bet anytime she wants, Sam can revert custody to Mom.

I had to get real.

There was no reason for them to love me.

Without a plan of where to go or whom I could call, I left my last class.

Suddenly, I regretted yelling at Sam. She didn't deserve me treating her like that.

From when we first met, she'd been super. She went looking for me when I ran away from the campground. She let me stay at her pretty house. She spent money on me and bought me clothes I liked. She let me fix up a room, she helped me paint it lavender, and let me use it like it was mine. She never hid me away when Jack came over. As if I was important to her, she took me places, talked to me, and listened to me.

Rather than being grateful, I was a disrespectful brat.

Feeling ashamed, I slowly left the building.

I was really happy to see Sam's car parked in the usual spot. I ran to it and opened the door. Before closing it, words of remorse flew from my lips. "I'm sorry."

She reached across the console for my hand. "It's okay. I'm sorry, too."

I summoned my courage. "If you want to kick me out, I'll understand."

Large tears fell from her eyes. "No matter what you say or do, I'll always love you and my home will always be your home."

Her words, like sunbeams straight from Heaven, warmed my heart. Not wanting the magical feeling to end, all the way to her house, I silently basked in the astonishing feeling.

Later while we were cooking, I said, "If you don't want me to date, I won't."

"I don't want to tell you what you can or can't do. I want you to be safe. I don't want anyone to harm you."

Even as I said, "I want you to be my friend," I realized that wasn't exactly true. I wanted her to be my real mother.

I shared, "It felt good for someone to like me enough to ask me out."

Sam dried her hands with a dishtowel and said, "Let's sit and talk." She walked to the couch and patted the space next to her.

I plopped down and started to cry.

She wrapped her arms around me.

After a while, I wiggled free. "I think you're right. I'm not ready to date. Besides he's too old for me."

The thoughts I had all day spilt out in a rush of words, "A few girls have boyfriends, but that's not what I want. I want to graduate and go to college. I want to make friends while I figure out a career I can enjoy. It might be nice to have a family of my own someday, but I think I have a lot to learn before I'm ready to become a mother. I can now understand why God took my baby. Maybe he'll send her back to me when I grow up and can be as good a mom as you."

I watched Sam wipe tears from her cheek. I knew my words touched her.

She said, "When did you become so wise? Most of us take the simple path like I did by avoiding people. As if I were a horse wearing blinders, I could sit in church week after week and not notice a soul. All the while, I wished I could be invisible.

"You helped me take notice of the richness around me."

She smiled. "Maybe we can grow up together?"

Falling back in her arms I told Sam, "I love that idea."

# Chapter Thirty-Three
## Sam

On the hot labor-day weekend with the threat of a thunderstorm, the high humidity made sleeping impossible. At five-thirty in the morning still lying in bed, I thought of how wonderfully things were progressing.

After visiting with her mother one afternoon, Charley told me. "Guess what?"

Before I could answer, she blurted, "I won't be seeing my mom anymore."

I held my breath fearing Mike had done something drastic. My expression must have revealed my fears.

She giggled. "Everything's fine. Mom's excited, because rather than taking her on vacation Mike's surprise was he'd secretly had his house up for sale. He recently accepted an offer. The money she'd saved will pay a moving van to take his possessions all the way to West Virginia. He picked the state, because he could purchase a house twice the size for half the price. He also felt good about leaving the den of sin in California and live in the heart of the Bible belt with people of his kind. Mom thinks she won't have to work or if she does, it'll only be part time."

"I'm sure you'll miss her."

"It won't be much different than now and with the cell phone you gave me we'll still be able to text each other. I figure Mike's charm must be wearing thin in Stockton. Before some girl rats on him, he's making a quick getaway. I'm only sad about him finding new victims in another place. I'm sure he's only taking my mom along as his cover so he can play the part of a devoted husband."

I sighed. "Guess you're relieved the threat of Mike cornering you will no longer be hanging over you like a storm cloud."

"Yep."

A few weeks later, Charley received a text from her mom raving about scenic West Virginia and the friendly folks at their new church. She showed me photos of the farmhouse Mike had purchased on twenty acres of land.

"Bet he likes not having close neighbors hearing what he likes to do best." She shuddered. "I just hope he doesn't work my mom too hard planting and picking vegetables."

To my delight, one day Charley assured me nightmares no longer plagued her. She declared, "The dreamcatcher really works. I can close my eyes and see nice things all night long."

Since her mother and Mike had moved to West Virginia, Charley was acting more and more like a typical teenager.

She began interacting with people her age. She invited friends to our home. Like her, they were responsible students, cheerful and respectful. She went to movies and shopped at the mall with them. She also continued attending our church's youth group.

I chuckled at the thought of her probably sleeping to eleven. Since her room was on the ground floor, two stories down from mine I felt it wise she still kept her door locked on the unlikely chance a burglar broke into the condo. But most of all, I was pleased her reason for doing so wasn't out of fear, but out of a normal desire to have privacy.

Jack and I were getting along extremely well. Like parenthood, our romance brought me to another unexplored joyful realm. To my amazement, with each passing day, my level of happiness increased. There were enchanting moments when just seeing his smile melted my heart.

Too antsy to stay in bed another second, I got up, took a shower, and quickly dressed in shorts and a casual top. As usual, I wasn't wearing shoes. Since dawn was breaking, I switched off the lights and felt my way through the dimness.

While in the hall, I heard a rustling sound.

Instinctively, I braced myself against the wall.

In the next instant, I admonished myself for overreacting.

*But what if someone has broken into the house? It's up to me to protect Charley.*

I slowly eased down the staircase and stepped into the kitchen.

Although the house was quiet, I felt uneasy. Without thinking, I opened a drawer and removed my loaded gun.

Turning it over in my hands, I laughed at my foolishness. Of course, there wasn't an intruder in the house.

I peered into the shadowy dining room. To improve my view, I flicked the light switch, but nothing happened. I glanced at the microwave oven and realized the green digital clock wasn't illuminated.

A sense of doom like an icy rain pricked my skin. Chilled to the marrow, I frantically ran to the opposite wall and tried another switch.

Like a scene from a horror movie, a dark figure suddenly emerged out of the shadows.

My heart leaped and a shrill cry flew from my throat.

A man with a stocking over his face came toward me. Through the thin fabric, I saw his bulging eyes.

Recognition assaulted me. I felt certain it was Charley's stepdad, Mike.

*Having only seen him from a distance, how can I be sure?*

*How can it be him? Haven't he and Charley's mom moved to the other side of the country?*

*Why would he risk arrest by coming here, by attacking me?*

I chided myself for buying into Charley's paranoia.

The intruder's garbled voice screamed over the other side of the kitchen island. "Did you think I'd let you get away with taking my daughter?"

It really was Mike. "Get out," I shrieked.

In an attempt to make him leave, or maybe out of panic, I fired off wild shots.

His long arm lunged and his large gloved hand knocked the gun out of my tight grip.

As if I were a ragdoll, he pulled me up over the granite surface and hurled me across the room.

My head hit hard on a cabinet door and the room spun around.

When I tried to sit up, intense dizziness made me swoon. My nauseous stomach seemed to be doing somersaults.

Mike came at me from all directions, kicking my side, stomping my legs, and punching my face.

Sharp pains overrode my queasiness.

His scratchy gloved fingers encircled my neck and squeezed the breath out of me.

My lungs craved air. I gasped and gasped a whole lot of nothingness until the space faded to blackness.

# Chapter Thirty-Four
## Charley

I awoke with a start surprised to see it was still night.

I vaguely remembered hearing strange noises.

Thinking the popping sounds were probably just a car rapidly backfiring, I relaxed.

But wasn't there a bang? Had Sam fallen off her stepstool while trying to get something from a high cabinet? Did she need my help?

I sat up.

Why was my heartbeat racing? Surely, if she wanted me she'd call out.

I calmed down by reassuring myself I'd had a bad dream.

I nestled my head on the pillow listening.

The house was quiet.

I closed my eyes. Not wanting to think of the terrifying days of the past, I focused on living in a safe place in the present. I knew I could trust Sam and Jack. They helped me believe my dreams would come true.

Suddenly, a cold sweat washed over me. Mike was still out there. It just wasn't like him to let me go without an argument, or threats of implied blackmail. He was vindictive. I remembered him saying many times how he never forgot when someone crossed him. One story was about a lady boss who'd fired him for being lazy. He said he walked away with his head high after telling her, "You can't fire me. I quit." Mom said he was only trying to scare us to keep us in line when he told us he patiently waited until she'd forgotten all about him. When she least expected it, wearing a ski mask, he hid in her garage overnight. Next morning when she was about to get into her car to drive to work, he brutally assaulted her.

I was sure one day he'd come after me, too. One day he'd make me suffer for walking out on him and embarrassing him to our church's congregation. By now besides hurting Mom, he probably had new playmates. Yet, he'd still want to get revenge for me disowning him as my dad. He'd still want to punish Sam for keeping me here.

He'd want to be the one to have the last word.

One day when I let my guard down, he'd attack me. He'd dump me beaten and damaged on the side of a road or in a ravine somewhere.

*What was that noise?*

I thought I heard a scream. I must've dozed off. Maybe I was dreaming it was me screaming like I did when Mike came at me.

With thoughts of Mike on my mind, it was easy to have a nightmare.

I told myself, "Just turn over and try to go back to sleep. The dreamcatcher will protect you and prevent you from having another nightmare."

# Chapter Thirty-Five
## Sam

From a non-feeling place, pain awakened me and transported me to the terrifying present.

My eyelids fluttered enough for me to see my gun across the kitchen floor.

Before Mike found Charley, despite the agony of moving I forced myself to slither toward the weapon.

My bruised hand reached for it.

*Did he believe I was dead? Is that why he carelessly left the weapon?*

Not sure of how many times I'd fired it, I checked the chamber.

Seeing it empty made my heart sink.

My pounding head couldn't think straight.

From fractured memories, I recalled a second gun stowed away in my bedroom closet. It'd been years since I placed it in the back of the top shelf.

Struggling to stand on my painful legs, I pressed my bleeding toes on the hardwood floors. As I went up the steps, I wondered where Mike was. Had he finished searching the upstairs of the house or would I find him lurking in the dark hallway.

I entered my bedroom washed in dawn's early light, opened the closet door, lifted my fingers but couldn't reach over the crowded space.

I hoped when Charley had discovered the gun, she'd put it back closer to the edge.

I pulled the chair from my vanity table over to the closet, stepped up and felt it wobble. I leaned one hand on the wall to regain my balance. With my other hand, I threw down long forgotten items until I reached the plastic box. I flipped the lid open and removed a .45. I jumped off the chair ignoring the harsh jolt to my weak ankles.

I searched drawers until I found my stashed ammunition. It took a few attempts for me to insert the clip in place.

When I heard a loud thud, a surge of energy propelled me through the hall. In my weary state, I pressed my weight on the banisher and slid down two flights of stairs to the lower level of my condo.

With light pouring in from the transom, I could see Mike's back aiming toward me as he swung a fireplace poker at a hole in Charley's bedroom door.

Without hesitation, I raised my gun. "Charley wake up, climb out the window. Get away before calling for help."

Mike shouted, "Not even a rabbit could fit through that puny window."

I warned him, "Get away from there or I'll shoot."

"Lady, it isn't loaded." He let out a cackle and spun around with the rod raised in a threatening position.

"Don't worry I'm not going to kill you 'cause when I finish with her I'll do you, too. And I'll be back again and again. And there's nothing you can do about it. You won't be able to prove a thing against me. I have an ironclad alibi now and will every time in the future."

Wielding the poker, he stepped in my direction.

My left hand gripped my right wrist. To steady myself, I took a deep breath. Not giving him time to take another step, while exhaling, my right index finger squeezed the trigger.

The gun made a loud blast.

As blood sprayed from his chest, his hair flared, his body wavered briefly before falling backward. When his head bumped one of Charley's guardian lions it toppled on its side.

Redness seeped from his shirt as his body lay perfectly still.

Frenzied anger prompted me to inch closer and bend over him. His frozen features convinced me he was gone. Overcome with an irresistible urge to kill my stepfather and every man who'd ever violated a child, I pumped out shots aimed at an opposite wall.

Spent by a feeling of vacant morbidity, I dropped my weapon.

Shifting my emotions from hate to love I shouted to Charley, "It's over. You okay?"

She didn't respond.

I threaded my fingers through the tiny broken space near the doorknob, reached in and unlocked the door.

Charlie was nowhere in sight.

I scanned the room and noticed the curtain blowing. Thankfully, she was able to climb out the window and jump into the garden below. Hopefully she was now in a place of safety.

In disbelief, I slithered down to the floor realizing I was a murderer. I'd broken one of God's most important commandments. A hollow emptiness intruded my momentary peace. I was worse than my stepdad, worse than Mike. I'd taken a life.

My body quaked with endless sobs until I felt Jack's arms wrap around me.

He whispered, "You're one brave soul."

I pushed him away. "I'm a killer. I murdered a man. I'm a monster."

He took my hands in his and gently squeezed them. "You were willing to give up your life for your child. There's no greater good."

I stared into his loving eyes. "Where's Charley?"

He said, "She's outside the house. She called, but by the time, I got here... I'm sorry I didn't get here sooner."

With Jack's help, I walked on my wobbly legs.

He led me out of her room. I tried to avert my eyes from Mike's body but couldn't erase the horrific image of him lying there dead because of my violence.

A police officer stopped us. "Ma'am, I have to ask you a few questions."

I confessed, "I killed him." The words condemned me to an inner hell. My stomach burned with remorse. Why hadn't I acted differently? Why didn't I just stop him by aiming for his legs?

A man dressed in a suit, piped up. "I'm Dr. Olinski, the coroner. The deceased has a bullet wound in his left shoulder, but the fatal blow came from a crack to his skull. From the blood streaks on the toppled stone statue, my preliminary guess is the victim must've lost his balance when you shot him. When his body fell, his head came down hard on the foo dog."

I glanced at the female lion resting on its side. Clutched in her hand was her cub. Still shocked, I said, "So the legend is true. The imperial dog is truly a guardian."

He smiled.

I felt a rush of relief. I'd stopped Mike, but ironically, he killed himself first spiritually by abusing others and now physically by falling.

The medical examiner turned to the police officer. "You can collect the facts after this lady has a chance to receive medical attention." He addressed me, "An ambulance is on its way."

With Jack's arms supporting me, I walked through the garage. He pressed the button to open the bay door. We passed my car before stepping out into the glaring sunlight.

Charley came running toward us.

The three of us embraced in a tight hug.

Jack said, "We're together now and I hope for always."

It was more than I expected or hoped a loving family would be like.

With our heartstrings entwined I felt certain we stood on the threshold of blissful possibilities.

# About E.B. Sullivan

E.B. Sullivan, PhD is a clinical psychologist who loves writing fictional tales. She draws inspiration from the amazing people she has met and the magnificent places she has visited. Her home, nestled in an enchanting California forest, is an idyllic setting to stir her imagination in penning creative stories, novellas, and novels.

**Social Media**

Website: http://www.ebsullivan.com

Facebook: https://www.facebook.com/ebsullivan1

Twitter: http://www.twitter.com/ebsullivan1

Amazon Author Page: viewAuthor.at/EBSullivan

# If you enjoyed this story, check out these other Solstice Publishing books by E.B. Sullivan:

## Short Stories

### Tainted Cross

While working as a forensic intern Regina tackles the task of investigating her best friend's death. As she uncovers startling information about his past, she finds herself faced with the moral dilemma of distinguishing right from wrong.

viewbook.at/TaintedCross

### Poet's Key

In fulfilling a New Year's resolution, under San Diego's sunny skies, Gina walks to work. While ambling down a deserted street she stumbles upon a homeless man who speaks in rhyme. Although not sure of his mental stability, she welcomes his friendship. During their unconventional relationship, Gina finds herself on an unfamiliar, unpredictable path to an uncharted destination.

viewBook.at/PoetsKey

### 99 Cent Deal

Following an abusive marriage, Ruth picks up the pieces of her life by working as a cashier at a 99-cent store. She enjoys being a generous and thoughtful person until one customer, a mysterious, gorgeous stranger, offers her a life altering future.

viewBook.at/99CentDeal

## Novels

### Tarot Haunting

Cassandra's surname, Visconti, traces back to one of the first tarot decks. The Visconti-Sforza tarot cards, created in the fifteenth century and used in parlor games, symbolically convey Judeo-Christian faith teachings. Hundreds of years later, the occult claimed the decks. Although Cassandra feels haunted by a phantom "tarot ghost" to tell the world about tarot's pathway to God, as a Catholic, she feels she should avoid the decks commonly associated with fortunetelling. Hired by a famous TV personality, Jared Ashbel, to research tarot and present her findings on a segment of his *Fact or Truth* series she faces tests to her Christian faith, struggles with her passionate temptation toward playboy Jared, and encounters profound opportunities to discover her true self.

viewBook.at/TarotHaunting

### Between the Vines

In her memoir, Lucia recounts poignant memories of life on a vineyard. She takes her first steps, experiences her first kiss, and learns primary lessons between the vines. Swept away by a passion to transform luscious grapes into superb wines, Lucia embarks on a romantic adventure laced with both tender and harsh realities. Cultivating grapes demands work, devotion, sacrifices, and expertise. Knowledge, timing and luck are necessary to make fine wines. Enlisting Old World philosophies and wisdom Lucia attempts to tackle personal and professional challenges.

viewBook.at/BetweentheVines

**Alaska Awakening**

A luxury Alaskan vacation turns into horror for three couples, who find themselves captives on a remote island in Prince William Sound for a thirty million dollar ransom. If their children don't pay, their chances for survival are slim. In the middle of despair, there is hope, forgiveness, and love—for their children, themselves, and each other.

viewBook.at/AlaskaAwakening

www.ingramcontent.com/pod-product-compliance
Lightning Source LLC
Chambersburg PA
CBHW060426260626
47161CB00005B/1799